For DR. [...] A[...]
Thanks for [...]

Rich R[...]

The Pain Game

Richard Rybicki

DEDICATION

For my wife Sharon. Thank you for loving me and
believing in me.

ACKNOWLEDGMENTS

I would like to express my gratitude to the many people who saw me through this book; to all those who provided support, talked things over, read, wrote, offered comments, and assisted in the editing, proofreading and design.

I would especially like to acknowledge Christie Sergo, my editor, and thank her for all her hard work and advice. Also, thanks to fellow author Robert Weisskopf for his encouragement and guidance.

Last but not least, I would like to thank the men and women of Law Enforcement, especially those of the Chicago Police Department, and the many I worked, laughed, and cried with over the years.

Table of Contents

CHAPTER ONE

He wore black. Shoe, pants, and shirt because that's what you do when you're committing a burglary. He pulled his car behind the building and positioned it between two large green dumpsters. He clicked off the headlights and cut the engine. Reaching for the backpack on the seat next to him he removed his laptop computer. He laid it on the passenger seat and checked the remaining contents. He zipped it closed and exited the car with the pack, leaving the laptop.

He walked around the back end of the car and approached a small frosted glass window to the right of the rear door. The window was about two feet square and its bottom sill about shoulder height from the ground. With a little squirming he knew he would fit through.

Taking a screwdriver from a side pocket of his pack he slipped the flat end between the sill and the sash. He took another quick look around the area and leveraged the window open. It opened easily. He had unlatched it earlier that day.

Replacing the screwdriver in his pack, he removed a small penlight and stuck it in his mouth. He pushed the pack through the open window and heard it drop to the floor inside. He grabbed the sill with both hands, hoisted himself up and slipped his upper body through the window. He plopped onto the tile floor being careful not to land on his bag.

Crouching below the window he waited for his eyes to adjust to the darkness. After a few seconds, when he began to make out the shapes of the fixtures in the room, he clicked on the penlight. He grabbed his pack, slung it over his shoulder, and closed the window. He moved across the room, through the door and into the hallway.

He made his way down the hall and found the door marked 'Exam Room'. It was written in black marker on a sheet of notebook paper taped to the door. He carefully opened the door and entered the small room. He placed his backpack on an old wood desk against the far wall. Pulling the desk chair into the center of the room, he stepped up on its seat. Using the penlight he began searching the ceiling.

As the penlight's beam finally focused on his objective, the room flooded with light, blinding him. He lost his balance and crashed to the floor, banging an elbow on the corner of the desk.

Lying on his back and shading his eyes with a hand, he looked up at the large man standing at the door. His hand was on the light switch. Shock turned to fear as the man rushed at him. He was flipped onto his stomach and his arms were pinned behind his back, putting more strain on his elbow. He whimpered in pain.

The man clamped his wrists in handcuffs and stood over him with one foot on his back. He grabbed the backpack off the desk and ripped it open.

"What the hell is this?" the man said.

CHAPTER TWO

I was in bed. The air was thick and damp but the sheets were cool. I was in that hazy middle ground where I thought I was asleep but I wasn't sure. My telephone rang. I buried my head in the pillow. It could be important. It could be my office. No, that wasn't possible. I rolled onto my back and covered my head with the pillow. I was slipping back into the fog. The phone's not ringing. I'm only dreaming.

The phone rang again, and then again. It wasn't a dream. I started coming to, placing myself. I remembered that I wasn't home, this was not my bed, and that was not my phone.

Through the door I heard my father answer the call. That's where I was, at my father's house. He didn't speak, or I couldn't hear him talking, I couldn't tell which. I began to doze again, until seconds later, or maybe it was minutes, he came into the room. He didn't knock.

He shook my shoulder. "Sam, wake up. You gotta go with me," he said.

Wherever it was he wanted me to go, I didn't want to go. I wanted to sleep. I liked sleep. Alone in my dark hole, I was safe and secure. I didn't have to think when I was asleep. I didn't have to remember. I told myself I was catching up. Recovering from all the double and triple shifts I would never have to work again. I was resting up and gathering my strength for the next great phase of my life that I was going to begin. The lie was easy.

"Come on, Sam," Dad said as he shook me again. "Get up. It's Josie's boy. You gotta come with." A dangling preposition, one of the classic earmarks of the Chicago accent. It was funny how it hurt my ears since I moved to Florida.

"Josie?" I mumbled.

"Yes, Josie, Sam. You remember, right? Her grandson Jerry is dead. You've gotta go to the morgue with me."

Twenty minutes later, after pulling on a pair of slacks and a button down shirt, I was with my Dad in his Cadillac on our way to pick up Josie.

I did remember her. I remembered meeting at the pool. It was a few months back, not long after I moved from Chicago to stay with him in Florida. He owned a small, two-bedroom cement-block home that he called a villa in a bayside complex on Siesta Key near the city of Sarasota.

On that morning I had dragged myself out of bed around noon, as I was getting used to doing, and plodded into the kitchen to make myself a pot of coffee. On the counter, next to the pot, was a sticky note written in Dad's hand. He called me a pasty Pollock and told me to meet him at the pool. I thought, what the hell, so I put on a pair of swim trunks and flip-flops and shuffled, coffee mug and newspaper in hand, over to the pool.

The pool wasn't far, located in the center of the property and surrounded by a ring of the cookie-cutter villas. I cut through the walkway between two villas and stepped through a gate and onto the pool deck at the very moment my dad was doing a cannonball into the water. The water erupted in a great fountain and made a sound like a subway train rushing through a tunnel. He broke the surface and swam toward a woman who was lounging on a chaise under a sun umbrella.

"Hey, Josie. Did you see that? How was it? Was that a good one?"

He sounded like a ten-year-old showing off for his mom. The woman looked up from the magazine she held, gave him a smile, and told him how impressed she was.

6

As I approached she tilted her head and looked towards me.

"Well, you must be Sam." she said with just the slightest drawl.

She was a stunning natural beauty with high cheekbones and deep blue eyes. Only her silver-grey hair, which was tied back in a ponytail, and a scant few smile lines betrayed her age. She was wearing a blood red bikini – yes, a bikini -- showing off a body any 30 year old would envy and which highlighted her bone-white complexion. My dad told me later Josie admitted to sixty-five but he thought she might be a little older.

Before I could answer I heard my dad walking over, wet feet slapping on the pool deck. "Josie, this is my son, Sam. Sam, Josie Manfred." He looked at me and he was beaming. I knew it was a "What do you think of me now?" smile rather than "I'm so proud of my son" look.

"Well of course he is, Bernard. Look at you two, you could be twins."

No one ever called my dad Bernard. He was Bruno, a nickname he'd had ever since I could remember and preferred over his given name. He would alternately cringe or berate anyone who called him Bernard, depending on who was doing the calling. He did neither to Josie.

I spent most of the afternoon by the pool, making small talk and being embarrassed at Dad's attempts to impress Josie with his athletic prowess and stories from his career. Josie, like an archetypal southern belle, laughed politely at his jokes, feigned interest in his stories and pretended to be impressed with his physical feats of daring in the pool. For the life of me I couldn't understand what she saw in my dad: a short, pot-bellied, under-read ex-cop from Chicago that, throughout his career, worked harder at avoiding work than the work itself would have been.

That last thought brought me back to the now. We arrived and, as we pulled through an open iron gate and drove along a lengthy stone paver driveway, I looked up at a huge bay-front Mediterranean style home and made a mental note to ask my father how Josie made her money. I said to my dad, "Tell me again why I'm here."

"I need you to talk to the morgue people, Sam. You know, find out what happened. You did that for 15 years."

"Twelve, Dad. I was a detective for twelve of my twenty. You were the police too."

"But I never dealt with this stuff, Sam. You guys in Homicide did it all the time. You know what questions to ask. Believe me, I would do this myself if I could. But Josie deserves better than I can do for her. Okay?"

"Okay, Dad." At least he could admit his lack of expertise to me. " So run it down for me. Josie got a call from the police this morning and they said what, exactly? "

"So they tell her…wait, here she comes. Let her tell it, okay? "

Josie was walking down the few steps from her front door and Dad jumped from the Cadillac. He hurried over and walked with her to the car, gently holding her around her shoulders, guiding her to the car. She walked slowly, head down, occasionally dabbing her eyes with a handkerchief.

Dad opened the back door and, as she glided into the seat I could see she was looking much more her age. She noticed me and nodded a hello.

"I'm so sorry for your loss, Josie." I said.

My dad jumped in, "I hope you don't mind but I asked Sam along. He's got more experience at this than me."

Well, he even gave me credit in front of Josie, I thought.

"Thank you, Bernard. I'm grateful for the help. Thank you, Sam."

Dad pulled the car out of the driveway and headed north, crossing the Intracoastal Waterway Bridge that connected the key and the mainland. I didn't have a clue where the Sarasota County Morgue was but Dad seemed to know the way.

I gave it a few minutes to see if he would ask Josie about the police call this morning. When it was obvious he wasn't going to ask her, I did.

"They were short and to the point." she said. "Very business-like. I guess it must be hard on them, breaking this kind of news to people." She looked at me and her eyes said she guessed I had made those notifications before.

"Yes," is all I said. I always thought a death notification was the hardest part of the job. I never called, though. I always did it in person. It was harder but it was the right thing to do.

"Well," she continued, "they told me they had found my grandson Jerry in my car. They found it parked in the marina lot downtown. The officer said it was a drug overdose and that I could get more information from the Medical Examiner's Office."

"Is that it? Did they give you any other details?"

"No, not that I can remember, Sam. Wait, I think the officer said a detective would be contacting me sometime soon."

That was standard operating procedure with accidental overdoses everywhere. Any suspicious, violent, or accidental death would go to the Medical Examiner for an autopsy to determine the cause and manner of death. The local police would also conduct an investigation. Sometimes accidents were not accidents, suicides were not suicides, and even homicides were not homicides. Most times, though, they were.

"Did your grandson…did you know that he was using drugs, Josie?"

"No, Sam. I didn't think he was. Oh, I caught Gerald smoking marijuana a few times in his room and he was actually arrested for possession once but that was years ago. I never had any reason to believe he used hard drugs. He had a hard time adjusting when his mother left and he moved in with me. There were problems, you know. His grades dropped, he got into fights at school and started hanging with the wrong crowd. You know, the typical things. We worked through that though. We worked very hard. For the last few years things have been very good. He has been an absolute angel. He graduated high school with a good grade point average and is even enrolled in college now. I also think he might have been seeing a girl."

"Do you know her name?"

"I'm sure he mentioned it but I just don't recall it right now. I would say it's probably in his cell phone, if that helps."

"Yes, we should probably talk to her. Did you know where your grandson was going last night, what time he left, and if he was meeting anyone? Like this girl, maybe?"

"No," she said looking down at her hands folded in her lap. "I feel so terrible. I didn't even know he went out. I made dinner for us and afterwards Gerald went to his room to study. I watched a little television and went to bed early."

Josie looked up at me and I saw the devastating hurt in her eyes.

"Sam, do you really think he could have been taking drugs without my knowing about it? Could I have been that ignorant? Can you help me? Can you and Bernard help me find out what happened to my Jerry?"

I sat back in my seat and caught the sideways glance from my father. He and I suspected the truth already, as we had seen it hundreds of times before. I couldn't say it yet though, so instead I said, "Yes, Josie. I'll find out what happened.

CHAPTER THREE

Leon Irsay sat at his kitchen table sipping a beer and occasionally tapping at the keys of the laptop in front of him. He was concentrating on the screen and the video images playing back. There were several such files on the laptop and five recordable DVD disks. Each disk contained several files as well.

He was surprised at the quality of the full color video and thought it was almost, but not quite, high definition. The images playing back were a bird's eye view of the examination room and all one could see were the tops of people's heads and only part of their faces. But that was good enough for him to be able to recognize Dr. Zingara and the occasional patient of the many on the video.

Leon's assessment was that the video wasn't really that damning in and of itself. It would seem to be a typical day in any typical physician's examination room. The accompanying audio track was another story. When he heard it, the audio didn't surprise him. He knew what went on at the clinic and, in fact, nearly everyone did. No, that was wrong. Nearly everyone *assumed* they knew what went on at the clinic. But they didn't really know. More importantly, they couldn't prove what went on in the examination room.

This video and audio could, however. Anyone watching and listening would have no doubt as to what was going on in the examination room of the Manasota Pain Management Clinic.

When the audio and video track had ended Leon pushed away from the table, crumbled his empty beer can and tossed it into the garbage bin in the corner of his small kitchen, ignoring the empty recycle bin next to it. He got another from his refrigerator, popped the top and took a long pull from it. He went back to the laptop and stared at the screen.

Leon could see the video was about five hours in length and, from the time and date stamp on the video image, that it was recorded in six different sessions over two days. He clicked and dragged using the track pad, punched more keys and the evidence was gone, deleted. Almost.

Leon knew enough about computers to know experts could still recover deleted files on the hard drive of a computer, files the owner had thought he had destroyed. He had learned that lesson the hard way and made a point to learn how to cleanse a hard drive permanently. What Leon had learned is a file isn't really erased when the user tells the program or operating system to delete it. What is deleted is only a reference to the location of that file on the hard drive.

He had taken a class at the local community college. He learned that a computer is like a library, and the files on the hard drive are like the books in that library. Libraries once had card catalogues and each book in the library was assigned to a card in the catalogue. In order to find the book you are looking for you need to look it up in the library's card catalogue. That card will direct you to the book's location in the library. Computers also have a 'card catalogue' and in older computers it was called the File Allocation Table or FAT. Newer computers use something called NTFS or New Technology File System. They're basically the same thing.

When a file is saved on the computer the computer finds any available open space and writes the file to that location. It then marks the file's location in the FAT or NTFS. When a request is made to retrieve the file the computer looks up the location in the FAT or NTFS and then knows where to find the file.

When a request is make to delete the file the computer merely deletes the file's reference 'card', leaving the actual file untouched but marking its location as available or as 'free space'. It would be the same as removing a book's card from the card catalogue but not removing the book itself. If a person knew their way around the library's file system they could find the book. It was the same with a computer file.

Leon knew the only way to truly destroy a file was to overwrite the hard drive and, in geek jargon, wipe it clean. The amazing thing was that this was a relatively easy operation and software was readily available to handle this task. Leon remembered reading news stories about child pornographers that were often caught because they failed to take this simple precaution. How stupid could they be, he thought.

Leon put his half empty can on the table next to the laptop and walked into the living room of his small house. He retrieved the software he purchased earlier that day, tore open it's box, removed the DVD and inserted it into the laptop. The computer whirled and buzzed a few times and eventually, after a few mouse clicks, the software began overwriting the laptop's hard drive. Thirty minutes and two more beers later the laptop's hard drive was a blank slate, with every file and the entire operating system permanently destroyed.

Leon took the plastic DVDs and tossed them in his kitchen sink. He doused them in lighter fluid and set a match to them. He knew, however, there may be more copies. There may be more hours of video he hadn't learned of yet.

Leon removed his new DVD, closed the laptop, and added his last empty beer can to the others in the trash. At his kitchen sink, he splashed cold water on his face, dried off with a wad of paper towels and pulled his cell phone from his pocket. He cleared his throat and punched '1' on the speed dial.

After several rings the phone clicked and a voice on the other end said "Speak."

Leon gave his report speaking crisply and succinctly. He explained the threat. However there were loose ends to clear up, three of them to be exact. He felt a bead of sweat trickle down his forehead.

The man on the other end spoke. "The others must be questioned. Do that. Find out if there are others beside those three and collect all video and audio files."

"Yes sir," Leon said.

"All the files," the man said, "And take no other action until we are sure we can obtain all the files. Do you understand?"

"Yes, Doc," he said, but the line had already gone dead. Leon closed his phone and put it back into his pocket. It was almost daybreak, too late to go out for another six-pack. He went into the bedroom, peeled off his clothes and tossed them on the foot of the bed. The metal frame creaked under his bulk as he plopped down. He drifted off quickly and slept soundly.

CHAPTER FOUR

The Sarasota County Medical Examiner's Office had its offices on Siesta Drive just off Tamiami Trail but the real work was done in the morgue of Sarasota Memorial Hospital.

I hadn't thought about it before, mostly because I didn't have to, but Sarasota County just didn't have the amount of Medical Examiner cases that would necessitate a stand-alone facility. I was used to the Cook County facility back home that serviced the City of Chicago and various suburbs surrounding the city. A single tough summer weekend could result in twenty or more bodies waiting to be autopsied. Not so with Sarasota County, so they contracted with the best hospitals in the area and rented their morgue to do autopsies and store bodies that were ME cases. Dad had learned this earlier when he called the Medical Examiner's Office for directions.

He parked the car in the high-rise garage, and we took a short walk across Waldemere Street to the main building. I got directions from a volunteer at the information desk who looked embalmed herself and told Dad and Josie to wait in the lobby for me. I told Josie if the ME needed an identification of the body or any other information from her I would come and get her. I figured there was no reason to put her through more than was necessary. Neither Josie nor Dad argued with me.

I walked a short maze of white terrazzo floors and green tiled walls until I came to a bank of elevators. I pushed the call button and, immediately, the doors to my right opened. I got on and punched two. When I got off a little while later a familiar odor enveloped me. The odor was rotting flesh mixed with chlorine and disinfectant. I almost smiled as I inhaled deeply. I knew that I missed it.

I followed my nose left and down a hallway through several turns and, finally, a set of swinging stainless steel doors into the morgue. I was in a small reception area that protected the living from seeing the dead by another set of swinging doors and a counter in front of it that stretched wall to wall, from left to right. A woman in green scrubs and white lab coat came through the swinging doors on the other side of the counter. She was staring at a clipboard in her hand and didn't seem to notice me.

She was tall, almost as tall as me, and slender, with skin the color of creamy caramel. Maybe she was black, or

Hispanic, or even Middle Eastern, I couldn't tell. Her hair, shades of brown and black, hung just below her jawline in ringlets of soft curls. They were almost dreadlocks but not quite. She had high cheekbones that gave her eyes an almost Asian look. She wore no makeup and didn't need any. She was more than beautiful and out of my league.

"Excuse me." I said, walking to the counter.

She looked up. "Sorry, I didn't notice you. LEO?"

"No. My name is Sam Laska. I'm here about Jerry Manfred. I assume he's here."

"Yes, he is, just brought in a few hours ago. But I wasn't asking your name. I meant, are you a Law Enforcement Officer? A L-E-O." She smiled. It was a really nice smile.

"Sorry. I didn't catch that. I am. I mean I was. I'm not anymore. Anyway, I'm here for a friend."

I looked at the nametag pinned to her lab coat. It read 'Gabrielle Jones – Morgue Assistant'.

She instinctively pulled at the coat, closing it over her scrubs.

"Gerald Manfred was your friend? I'm sorry for your loss."

"No, not him. I never met him. I'm here for his grandmother. She got a call from the police and I came along to help her."

"Oh, okay. How can I help?" She came around from behind the counter, flipping a section of the countertop that stretched over a cutaway just for that purpose.

"Well, for starters, do you need her to make an identification? I'd hate to put her through that."

"I don't think we'll need her to do that. He had identification in his wallet, a driver's license and school ID. Also, he'll be fingerprinted. I was just about to do that. Do you know if he's ever been arrested?"

"Yes, his grandmother told me he had been."

"Where from?" she said, turning away for a moment as she picked up a pen from the counter and flipped through the papers on the clipboard.

"I don't really know. Somewhere around here, I guess."

"No. I mean you. Where did you work?" she looked up from her clipboard and smiled again.

"Chicago, the Chicago Police Department." I said. "I did twenty years there, most of it as a detective."

"Homicide, I guessing."

"Mostly, but I also worked sex crimes and some property crimes before that. How could you tell? I mean, do I look that much like a cop?"

"It's the way you carry yourself. And it's the smell."

"I smell like a cop?" Now I smiled.

"No, silly. This place." She smiled back. "It doesn't bother you.

"I've been in a few morgues, but never on the second floor. Usually the morgues are in the basement."

"No basements here in Florida. Water table is too high and the soil's not right."

"I never thought of that." There was a moment of uncomfortable silence until I said, "Can you tell me anything about how and where he was found? My friend said the police officer that phoned her called it an overdose."

"The autopsy hasn't been done yet, I only finished prepping his body for it. I'm waiting for Dr. Cortez to show up. He's the pathologist and the county Medical Examiner. The paperwork that came with the body says that's the suspected cause of death, though."

"Can you tell me why they think so?"

"I'm not supposed to discuss any reports with family or friends." She tilted her head and smiled again. It was a different smile this time, more of a 'we're members of the same club' smile. "But I'm betting I can trust you not to tell on me." She checked the papers on her clipboard again and, reading from one, said, "Victim found in backseat of an auto registered to one Josephine Manfred. Your friend?" She looked up at me and without waiting for an answer, continued, "No outward signs of violence, body cool to the touch. Traces of a foamy discharge from the mouth." She flipped to another page. "And several pills, looks like six total, found on the back seat and floor of the car. Suspected oxycodone."

She continued staring at her clipboard and frowned.

"Something else?" I asked.

She paused a few seconds and said, "No, that's it. But that's a little strange."

"Why?"

"Did you ever work narcotics? Do you have any experience with oxy users?"

"No, not really. I don't ever recall running across it. It's a type of synthetic morphine, isn't it?"

"More like synthetic heroin. Oxy users generally will crush the pills and snort the powder or cook the crushed pills like heroin and inject it. I've even heard some users will smoke the pills, like crack cocaine. According to these reports no 'works' – syringes, cooking spoons, pipes and the like – were found. Plus, I found no powdery residue around the nostrils."

"So that would leave oral ingestion." I said.

"Yes, that's all that's left, but it's unusual for oxy junkies. They usually prefer a more direct route to their high. My preliminary inspection of the body shows no signs of long-term abuse. No extreme weight loss, track marks or the like, so we might assume he was a newbie. Maybe he was just getting high for the first or second time and made a miscalculation on the dose. It happens."

"So, it is what it is." I said.

"Probably. We'll know more after the autopsy. That's why we do 'em."

She looked back to her clipboard and flipped through a few more pages.

"This report says detective King was on the scene. You may want to talk with him. If he can't add anything else, he'd still be the one to see about getting your friend's personal effects and car back. It says here he ordered the car towed. I know him, he's a bit surly but a good guy down deep."

I was about to thank her when a short, olive-skinned man in an off-white linen suit came through the same swinging doors as I did. He was moving with a purpose until he saw me standing with Gabrielle Jones. A slight frown, nearly imperceptible, came to his already stern expression.

"Five minutes, Ms. Jones." he said and then continued to the back room, quickly flipping the counter at the gap, and pushing through the second set of doors.

"Did I cause you a problem?" I asked.

"He doesn't like me on this side of the counter, but don't worry, I can handle him."

"I'll go then, thanks for all your help. Can I call later, after the autopsy, to confirm the OD?"

"Well, the toxicology results will take at least a week, but I'm sure Doctor Cortez will make a preliminary finding. Instead of calling why don't we meet tonight after I get off? I can fill you in on any details then."

"You don't have to do that. You've helped a lot already." I said.

"I'm going to a great tapas restaurant, Ceviche, on First Street, just east of Tamiami Trail. They have a rooftop bar. Meet me there around six-thirty, before sunset."

"Thanks, but I shouldn't intrude on you and your friends. I'll just call."

"I'm not meeting any friends there. It'll just be you and me." She smiled again and I hesitated while my mind processed that.

"Wait. Are you asking me out?"

"Well, Sam Laska. You really were a detective," she said. She turned and walked through the counter into the back and gave me one last smile over her shoulder before disappearing through the doors.

CHAPTER FIVE

Lindsey punched the screen of her phone and dialed the number for the fifteenth time this morning. She prayed he would answer. He didn't and she frowned as the call went directly to voicemail without ringing. There was no sense leaving another message and she snapped her phone shut after checking the time. She slipped the phone into the hip pocket of her jeans, readjusted the backpack she had slung over her left shoulder, and hurried off to class. Maybe he forgot to charge his phone or maybe he lost it. She didn't want to think there could be another reason he didn't call.

###

We got back to Josie's house a little before noon. I didn't say much in the car except that the post mortem exam was not yet done and we would have to wait for a definitive answer. I also told Josie I had learned the name of the detective handling the case, and I would talk to him and see about her grandson's property and her car. Josie thanked me and excused herself to go lie down. She seemed to have aged twenty years since this morning.

I told my dad he should stay with Josie and, again, he didn't argue. I started to tell him when Josie feels better he should get her thinking about funeral arrangements, but he gave me a look and I backed off.

After checking the address with Information on the phone, I took Dad's car and headed to the City of Sarasota Police Department. It was a brand new facility on Adams Lane east of Washington Street. I parked in the public lot and was walking through the front door less than a minute later.

I stood at the front desk until a police officer that had been on the phone finished with his call and gave me a look over his reading glasses. I asked to see Detective King and explained my business. I showed my identification and signed a log and was told to wait in the lobby until Detective King was available.

Ten minutes later I was seated in a metal desk chair with a torn leather seat that was obviously missing a major portion of its stuffing. I guessed the cost of the new building busted the budget and there was no money left for new furniture.

The man seated across from me, behind an equally distressed metal desk with a wad of paper stuck under one leg and a stack of files in an in-basket, was Detective King. He was a large man but carried it well, like a defensive lineman, though his shoulders were stooped and every movement he made seemed to be a chore. I figured it was more from the weight of his caseload than his advancing age. His hair was black but had a patch of gray over each ear and his deep brown skin was shiny with perspiration. The brass nameplate on his desk said 'Det. Nosmo King'.

I smiled and when I looked up he was staring at me, arms folded across his chest as he leaned back in his chair.

"Don't bother, I've heard them all," he said.

"I don't know what you're talking about." I lied and stopped trying to think of a snappy line.

He sat upright and moved his bulky frame closer to the desk. "And how are you related to the deceased, Mr. Laska?" he said, pulling out a cheap pen from the inside pocket of a sport coat that looked one size too small on him.

"I'm not. I'm a friend of his grandmother. She's pretty shaken up. The boy lived with her, his parents are out of the picture, I guess. I'm helping her out."

"Okay, I get it. What can I do to help?"

"First, thanks for seeing me. Second, you were on the scene I was told. Can you tell me what happened?"

"Without getting into too much detail, it's a typical overdose. He was found in the car, dead in the backseat. The car was parked in the far south end of the lot at the Marina. Oxycodone pills strewn about the car. We see plenty of these lately, about two or three a month."

"That's a lot?" Again I was used to the big city where overdoses were almost as common as corrupt politicians.

"For a small town like this, sure. We average eleven oxy related deaths a month in Florida. That's a bunch. If eleven dead dolphins were found on the beaches every month people would be calling for a State and Federal investigation. But people don't give a damn when it's junkies."

He was right about that. It's natural to think it's the junkie's own fault and that a junkie deserved it or sealed his own fate by becoming an addict. "Can I ask who found the body?"

"I can't give you details like that. I know it's hard for some people to accept but these things happen. When the results of the autopsy come back I'm confident we'll get confirmation. It's best to accept it and move on."

31

"Please don't give me that load of crap," I said. Nosmo King looked sharply at me. "I've recited that same rehearsed speech hundreds of times." I dug into my wallet, pulled out my identification card from the city and handed it to him. It was exactly the same as the current ID cards except mine was stamped with a big red 'RETIRED'. "I worked Homicide in Chicago and I know exactly what this is too. My friend asked me to help her out. You know how it is. She can't believe the kid was a user, blah blah blah. I just want a few details so I could ease her mind. You know, make it a little easier for her to accept. How about it?"

He took my ID and looked it over carefully, examining both sides, as if he really knew what a Chicago Police ID card looked like.

"Chicago, huh? I've been there. Well, passed through anyway. I didn't care for the looks of the place. You're a little young to be retired, aren't you?

"Yeah, I guess. I just couldn't take it any longer, I burned out, so I retired," I lied. "So, how about it? Can we talk?"

"Okay, big city detective, I guess we can drop the horseshit. But you should have told me up front you were on the job."

I let that 'big city detective' bit of condescension go and said, "Thanks," as he handed me my ID card. "I probably should have led with that. So, who found the body?"

Nosmo King sat back in his chair again and let out a sigh. "We don't know. It was an anonymous call. When the first officer arrived on the scene he found the victim in the car, passenger's side window broken and the keys in the ignition, turned off. We think it was some bum, I guess they call them homeless people nowadays, called it in. There are plenty of them that hang around the marina. It's not a heavily patrolled area and that makes it easy to break into a car or boat for a comfortable place to sleep."

"So, you think a homeless person looking for a place to sleep broke the car window, found the body, and then called it in?"

"That's the theory."

"Where did he call from? Are there public phones nearby?"

"Actually, the call came from the victim's own cell phone. We found it on the front seat along with a backpack."

"Was anything in the backpack?"

"Nothing of any value, just some pens, papers and the like. School stuff, it looks like."

"Did you have the phone fingerprinted?"

"No, we didn't bother." King noticed a growing look of disgust on my face and added, "The officer that responded handled the phone. I know he made a mistake, but come on. This is an obvious OD."

"Yeah, well, there are a few things starting to concern me. I understand the victim had a wallet. Did he have any money on him?"

"Yeah, his wallet was in his back pocket and he had, let's see." King shuffled a few papers on his desk until he found the one he needed. "Twelve dollars. A ten and two singles."

"So, a homeless person looking for a place to sleep breaks the car window, finds the body in the backseat, and now decides to be a good citizen. He calls the police on the victim's cell phone that he conveniently finds in the car and then leaves without stealing the cell phone, which is probably worth a few bucks in pawn. Nor does he go through the victim's pockets or even take the pills which have got to be worth, what, ten bucks each?"

The expression on Nosmo King's face hardened and he folded his arms across his big chest again. "That's my theory. Maybe he didn't see the pills or the body spooked him. It ain't every day he's gonna find a body in a car. Again, retired detective Laska, overdoses like this are pretty common. If it walks, talks, and shits like a goose it probably is a goose. Don't you think?"

My experience told me he was right. But it bothered me that someone who had no qualms about busting out a window to sleep in someone's car would not steal from them as well. Maybe there was a better class of homeless here in Florida, but I didn't think so.

"I think you still have some investigating to do." I said.

The detective unfolded his arms and placed his hands, palms down, on his desk. He leaned forward slightly and said, "This case is all but over. I'm going to wait for the autopsy, the results of which I can easily guess, and then I'm going to type a report explaining what a tragedy it was. Another young, promising life snuffed out and lost to drugs. And then it'll be done with, closed. Nothing more than an accidental overdose. I haven't got the time to waste because a big city dick thinks he knows more than us dumb, small town, countrified, cracker polices." He pronounced it 'PO-leeses'.

"Come on, don't you think there're a few questions that still need answering?" I said. "At least try to find your anonymous caller and find out what he knows."

"I said this case is done. We are too. I'm busy and I have a lot to do, so if you don't mind?"

I understood where the detective was coming from. He was probably right and if I were doing the investigation, I might do the same; but I had a little tingle growing in my gut telling me otherwise. Though I was aggravated and felt my blood pressure rising I didn't want to leave King angry. I stood and said, " Okay, it's not my place to question your investigation. I'm sorry. You're probably right, it's probably nothing more than an accidental overdose." It killed me to say it.

Nosmo King sat back and said, "Yeah, sure. No problem. And I am right."

I remembered to ask about Jerry's personal property and Josie's car. King found the right paperwork and again, after he made a copy of my identification, I signed multiple forms for the small bag of Jerry's property and Josie's car. I was surprised I didn't have to sign for the pen I borrowed to sign the forms.

When I got back to dad's Cadillac I opened the manila bag of property and spilled it out onto the seat next to me. Lying on the seat was a black leather wallet containing a driver's license, a college ID from Middle South Florida University, a few odd pieces of paper and notes, and twelve dollars; forty-two cents in change; a steel ring with two keys; and a cell phone. The cell phone was one of those fancy smart phones and was turned off. No one wanted to hear constant ringing from cell phones in the property room.

Cell phones could be a wealth of information and I was anxious to check the contact list. Maybe one or two of them, especially a girlfriend, could help me piece together what happened to Jerry and bring some measure of closure to Josie. But I didn't want to poke around in Jerry's phone without Josie's permission so I left it alone.

Josie's car, the paperwork said it was a pearl white Infinity G37 four-door, was at a lot a few miles north and just west of Washington Street. I couldn't pick it up without another driver so I started back to Josie's house to get my dad. Ten minutes later I was midway across the north bridge that connected the mainland with Siesta Key ignoring the afternoon sun glinting off the blue waters of Sarasota Bay. Yawning, I looked at the dashboard clock. It was two-thirty, my naptime.

CHAPTER SIX

"Miss Wellington?"

Lindsey was lost in her thoughts and didn't hear the Professor.

"Miss Wellington? Would you care to join the discussion?"

Joel Gibson, the student in the seat next to her, nudged the back of her seat. Lindsey sat upright, her attention refocused on her professor, but she was lost. Professor Canby knew it too.

"We were discussing objectivity in journalism and whether it is truly possible for a journalist to be objective considering every human being has their own biases and preconceptions based on their individual life experiences. Do you have anything to add?" he said.

"I'm sorry, Professor." Lindsey said, "My mind was elsewhere." Lindsey, and the rest of her classmates, knew not to make excuses. Professor Douglas Canby did not tolerate excuses because, as he explained, excuses were nothing more than attempts to justify failure.

"Yes. It was on the telephone in your lap," he said. "Please put it away and pay attention."

Lindsey did as she was told and put her phone in her pocket but she couldn't pay attention. Jerry hadn't shown up in class like she had hoped and she was worried. She talked to Joel, that little wimp, before class and told him she hadn't yet heard from Jerry.

"He was supposed to call you right after." Joel said, as if she didn't remember or was too stupid to have understood the plan.

"I know that, Joel. Why do you think I'm so worried?"

"We have a meeting with the professor right after class. What are we going to do if Jerry doesn't show up?"

"I don't care. I'm more worried about Jerry. Aren't you?"

"I'll bet he overslept. Yeah, I'll bet that's what happened. That lazy bastard overslept and we're going to take heat from Canby because of it."

"I don't think he overslept. He said he'd call last night and he didn't. I've been trying him all morning and his phone just goes right to voicemail. That's not like him, he never turns his phone off. He even uses it as his alarm

Richard Rybicki

clock. I'm afraid something might have happened and I don't know what to do."

"For chrissakes, Lindsey, nothing happened. Jerry's just unreliable and lazy and we're going to be the ones that suffer. I knew we shouldn't have brought him in with us. I shouldn't have listened to you."

"Don't give me that. You wanted him too. And probably because you were too afraid to do the dirty work yourself."

Joel shushed her when two other students took seats near them. "We'll talk later. If Jerry misses class don't say anything to Canby. Let me do the talking." Joel stood up and gave her a look with squinted eyes and a furrowed brow, which was probably meant to reinforce the seriousness of his position but only made him look like a spoiled toddler. He grabbed his book and notepad and moved to the seat behind Lindsey.

Professor Douglas Canby was the head of the Scott School of Journalism at Middle South Florida University and had the reputation as a demanding instructor. The class he was teaching this semester, Journalistic Ethics, was a requirement and was rarely offered so Lindsey made sure she was enrolled. She also convinced Jerry to jump on it. If they wanted to graduate on time they couldn't chance missing it.

Lindsey had taken a class taught by Canby last semester and believed Canby deserved his reputation as both a tough instructor and a poseur. He dressed as he thought a journalism professor should, usually wearing scuffed loafers, rumpled khakis, a blue button-down shirt, and a brown tweed sport coat with leather patches on the elbows. Wire-framed bifocals and a soul patch, a little scruff of hair just below his bottom lip, completed his look. He also never failed to mention to each class he taught that he had once been nominated for a Pulitzer Prize.

Despite Lindsey's opinion of his personal style, she was surprised and honored when Canby approached her and invited her to be part of a new project he was forming. He explained it was to be an exciting undertaking and give her and her teammates real world investigative journalism experience. If successful it would rock the political and medical foundations of Florida. Aside from that, he practically guaranteed her an internship with a local television station for the summer. She couldn't say no.

The project turned out to be everything Canby promised and Lindsey saw it's potential to make a name for everyone involved. The work was hard and risky at times, and that made it exhilarating. She never really thought anything bad would happen though. But, now, she hadn't heard from Jerry and believed he might be in trouble. She was worried.

When the class ended, Professor Canby remained at the lectern in the front of the room, shoveling papers into his worn brown leather book bag. Lindsey had stayed in her seat, waiting for the other students to file out and making sure none lingered to suck up to Canby with stupid questions. She intended to stay seated in the hope that Canby would ignore her and Joel and walk out the door, but Joel poked her again and walked over to Canby.

"Professor Canby," he said, "Is our meeting with you still on?"

Canby continued shuffling papers and flipping through pages of a textbook and, without looking up, said, "One minute, Gibson."

It was a full five minutes later when Canby finished, having placed all his papers and books into his bag and snapping it closed with the brass plated clasp. Putting the bag on the floor he turned to Joel and Lindsey, who had joined him at the front of the room. He leaned an elbow on the lectern and looked at Lindsey with raised eyebrows, "I did not see Mr. Manfred in class today."

Lindsey looked down at her feet and was about to speak when Joel jumped in.

42

"He probably just overslept. He must have turned off his cell phone. We can't get hold of him."

"Did you try his home phone?"

"No, sir." Joel said, and turning to Lindsey, "We don't know it, right Lindsey?"

Before she could answer, Professor Canby turned to Joel and said, "If you cannot contact Mr. Manfred you do not know why he is absent. Just state the facts. Don't make excuses, Mr. Gibson". And then to both Joel and Lindsey he said, "Mr. Manfred should have been here. His absence reflects badly on all of you. Although he is a mediocre student you both vouched for him and that is why I allowed him to be involved in this project. Your grade for this class is dependent on the successful outcome of the project and that means each of you is dependent on the others."

Lindsey caught Joel scowling at her and shot a look right back at him.

"That being said," Canby continued, "you must determine the cause of Mr. Manfred's absence. If, as you said Mr. Gibson, it is due to a purely mundane reason, I will allow you two to deal with it. However, if there is a more critical basis for his absence, we may need to do some damage control."

"I'm sorry, sir." Lindsey said, "I don't understand."

"Ms. Wellington, if Mr. Manfred failed to complete his assignment it may be due to the intervention of forces which would necessitate shielding the university and myself from embarrassing accusations, or worse, liability. In short, we must make sure he keeps his mouth shut."

"That's what I'm worried about, sir. What if something happened to Jerry?" Lindsey said.

"That possibility exists, Ms. Wellington. But we all knew the risks when we undertook this project. I believe I explained them thoroughly, did I not?"

"Yes sir, but…"

"Please contact me via email when the question of Mr. Manfred's absence is answered," Canby said, picking up the book bag at his feet, " You might try knocking on his door this time. And again, as always, speak of this to no one. We all understand the consequences should anyone…should you be found out."

Professor Canby turned and walked out the door as Lindsey and Joel stood and watched him.

Lindsey stood staring at the door, "Did you hear him?" she said. "He couldn't care less about Jerry, or either one of us."

"No, he's just telling it like it is. Welcome to the grown-up world of responsibility." Joel said.

Lindsey turned to him and said, "You're an ass."

She walked back to her seat and gathered up her notebook and pen. She put them in the backpack she slung over her left shoulder. She walked out of the room without a single look back at Joel, even when he called out, "So, you'll keep checking on Jerry?"

CHAPTER SEVEN

It was afternoon already and Leon had barely slept, catching only a few hours. He took his time getting ready, showering, shaving, and dressing in no rush at all. Class wasn't for an hour and a half and the campus was only a short drive away. While he ate his breakfast over the sink, dry toast and orange juice straight from the carton, he began planning his day based on what he learned the night before.

It was hard understanding the kid, being all doped up like that, sitting in the Doc's chair, drooling on himself and eyes almost rolled to the back of his head. Eventually though, with a little patience, he got what he needed.

At first the kid wouldn't cooperate. Even though Leon could see he was afraid, he wouldn't talk. He said he had a right to remain silent even after Leon told him he wasn't a cop and it didn't work that way.

"If you're not a cop then you must be some kind of security guard and it's the same thing. I don't have to incriminate myself," he said.

"Boy, I don't need you to incriminate yourself. I know what you did. I was here when you broke in. I also think I know why. I thought it was to steal pills at first but it wasn't, huh?" Leon said.

The kid tried to be a hard case, staring at him with no expression, so Leon continued.

"When I saw that stuff in your backpack, it didn't click right away. I thought what the hell were you doing with that? But then, when I picked one up and saw it was a camera, I knew. Where do you get things like that anyway? Who makes a smoke detector camera?"

Again, the kid said nothing. Leon hoped for an answer he knew wasn't coming because he really wanted to know. He walked over to the desk and picked up the clandestine camera. He turned it over in his hands, examining it. He turned back to the kid when he heard a grunt and the clink of his handcuffs. The kid was straining to pull a hand free and had a pained look on his face.

"Arm hurts, huh? Don't bother fidgeting, I've got them tight around the bone." Looking back to the device in his hand he said, "I can see the camera is battery operated. That must be why you're here tonight, huh? The battery crapped out and you came to change it out." The kid stopped pulling against the handcuffs and stared at Leon again.

"Yeah, I know." Leon said, staring back. "You, or someone you're working with, were here last week. I found the unlocked window in the bathroom and scuff marks on the wall. Funny thing was, we couldn't find anything missing. No pills, no hypes, no prescription pads, nothing. I had to convince Doc to lock me in overnight when I found the window unlatched again. I guess I was right, huh?"

The kid kept his poker face but his shoulders slumped just enough for Leon to know he got it right.

Leon went back to the camera. "There's no recording device on the camera, nothing in the ceiling, so that must mean wireless transmission. Over the internet, right?" Leon was talking more to himself than the kid. Leon looked over to the kid and saw him staring at the floor. Leon had it right again.

"Well, let's get to it then." Leon said. He put the camera on the desk and picked up the wallet he had taken out of the kid's pocket along with his car keys and cell phone.

Flipping it open he examined its contents: a driver's license and school ID, an odd assortment of paper scraps with notes and phone numbers, and several photographs. He stuffed it all back into the wallet then moved on to the cell phone, going over the contact list and the recent calls.

Leon grabbed another chair and sat opposite the kid. "Which of these people am I interested in, Jerry?" Leon said, "Or do you want me to call you Gerald?"

His head still hung low, Jerry Manfred said nothing.

"Jerry it is, then. Listen, Jerry, you're obviously very interested in what we do here. I don't exactly know why so you're gonna tell me. I also don't think you're working alone so I gotta know who else you're working with. You're gonna tell me that, too."

"I'm not going to tell you anything so just go ahead and take me to jail." Jerry said, still staring at the floor.

"You misunderstand, Jerry. You're not going to jail, no police are gonna be involved here, and you're gonna tell me what I want to know. In a few minutes you won't be able to stop yourself from talking." Leon stood up and, with his foot, shoved his chair off to the side. He walked over to a cabinet on the wall opposite the desk and opened the top compartment. Jerry watched him as he rooted around and withdrew a syringe, needle and small bottle of amber liquid.

Sticking the syringe's needle into the cap of the inverted bottle, Leon turned to Jerry and said, " You're going on the ride of your life, Jerry."

Jerry, beginning to understand what lie ahead, was as frightened as he had ever been in his life but still managed a "Fuck you" to Leon.

CHAPTER EIGHT

I rang the bell and was let into Josie's house by my dad. He led me through the marble tiled foyer into the large living room. Josie was sitting on a blue velvet covered sofa slowly turning the pages of a photo album she held in her lap. She looked up at me, her eyes begging for an answer. There was none, not yet anyway, and I told her so.

"I talked to the detective handling the case and he believes Jerry died from an accidental overdose. He seems convinced but will wait to close the case until the Medical Examiner makes his determination."

"What about you, Sam? What do you think?" Josie asked.

I wasn't sure myself and I told her so. "I don't know what to think, Josie. There are many signs that point to an accidental overdose. In fact, Jerry's death seems to be a prototypical OD. But there are a few things that bother me, and if you don't mind, I'm going to check them out."

"Please, Sam."

My dad, who had walked to the sofa and sat next to Josie, said "What things, Sam? What did you find out?"

I looked at Josie. Her eyes, red and swollen, were glued to me. I turned back to dad and stared at him, hard. I didn't want to discuss this in front of Josie, give her false hope, and I thought he should know that.

I took a deep breath, let it out slowly and then told them what Detective King told me: How Jerry was found with his phone and money, the broken car window, the anonymous phone call, and the pills. "But", I said to Josie, "just because nothing was taken doesn't mean it's not an OD. It could, and very likely, mean nothing. Detective King thinks so, and maybe he's right. I don't like loose ends so I'll poke around a bit."

I handed Josie the envelope of Jerry's things. She didn't open it.

"Jerry's phone is in there. I'd like to go through the list of contacts and recent calls if it's okay with you. And I'm going to ask you not to touch the phone until I go through it. Information could get accidently destroyed. But first, I'll take Dad and we'll pick up your car." Looking over at him I gave him a curt "Let's go."

As I turned and walked to the door I heard my dad say to Josie, "Will you be okay if I go? It'll only be a little while."

I felt like shit. I didn't even consider leaving Josie alone and was more concerned with letting my dad know I was miffed at him. But instead of stopping and apologizing I continued on through the door and waited in the car for Dad. I sat there feeling like an even bigger shit for that.

A few minutes later we were on our way, heading back over the North Bridge towards the city. We didn't talk much, only a few short "turn here's" and "I know the ways". Though I had lived in Sarasota only a few short months I was no stranger to the area and I knew my way around pretty well. Dad had been living here since he retired some years ago, living in the place he and mom bought before I could remember. They had bought it as an investment and as somewhere they could both retire to and escape the Chicago winters. They rented it out during 'the season' – Christmas through Easter - and we vacationed there most summers, usually the entire month of August.

It was as hot as hot gets and the humid air stuck to you like moss. But, being a kid, I didn't care as long as the beach or pool was nearby. Mom loved the place. I couldn't tell if it was the beach, the villa, or just the carefree feeling of being on vacation with her family that made her so joyful. Whatever it was she always seemed happiest when we were there.

Then, one year, she got sick. I was a junior at the
University of Illinois. She was diagnosed with breast
cancer. By the time it was discovered it had spread to her
lymph nodes and bones and she died two months later.
Dad took it hard. He spent more and more time at home,
taking all the vacation days he could. He retired the week I
graduated. He sold everything except his car and moved
into the villa mom loved so much. I took the test for the
police department and a job as a janitor at my old grammar
school. The CPD called a few months later and I followed
in Dad's footsteps. Well, not quite. I actually did police
work.

When mom died, I was mostly numb. It hurt but I
never cried. I missed her deeply but I didn't know how to
let it out, I didn't know how to grieve. My mother was the
first person I ever knew that died.

"How much farther?" Dad said. We were on
Washington Boulevard heading north and passing
Seventeenth Street. The lot of The Hob Nob Drive Inn on
the northwest corner was packed with cars. The smell of
wonderfully greasy burgers and fried onions filled the car
and my stomach growled. The clock on the dashboard
read 3:20 and I hadn't eaten since dinner the day before.

"Another mile or so." I said, "It's just the other
side of MLK Way, on Myrtle."

At the mention of Martin Luther King Way, and out of the corner of my eye, I saw dad check his door lock. I didn't want to start that whole argument again so I sighed to myself and let it go. Ten minutes later we pulled into the driveway of the tow yard.

It was a large lot, taking up a full quarter of the block at least, and surrounded by an eight-foot chain link fence topped with razor wire. The entrance gate, two large sections of swinging chain link fence, was closed. A heavy chain was wrapped around the middle supports of both gates and secured with a padlock the size of a sixteen-inch softball.

I switched off the car, gave my dad the keys, and asked him to wait until we knew for sure I could get the car and it was drivable. I walked up to the gate and, looking through the chain link, saw no one. In the middle of the lot was a small building, or a large shack – the perspective depending on whether you were inside or outside of it – painted a putrid shade of olive green. There was a single door facing the gate and an ancient air conditioner hanging out of a window on the side. There were scars and scrapes of various colors along the entire side of the shack I could see, all about bumper high.

Figuring there must be a way to attract the attention of whomever may be around I scanned the entire gate and adjoining fences. Off to the right, tied to the fence with wire, was a small square of plywood that someone hand-lettered and read 'Push bell for service'. Below that someone had written in black marker 'only once!' I spied an old brass push-button doorbell attached to the sign and, following orders, punched it once.

A loud clanging sound came from somewhere in the back of the lot. The bell sounded like an old school bell or maybe a firehouse bell. It was loud enough to make me jump and my father yell "Christ!" through the closed windows of his car.

The door to the shack opened and a young kid, maybe he was twenty or so, came out and started a slow amble towards the fence. He wore faded jeans, rips in both knees, and a dark blue, long sleeved work shirt. The sleeves were rolled up to mid-forearm. A patch sewn onto his left chest said 'Andy'. His work boots, once black, were scuffed into untold shades of grey.

He stopped about ten feet short of the fence. "What do you need?" he said.

"I'm here to pick up a car. Police towed it here last night from the marina."

"You got the release?" He combed his fingers through long, stringy hair pushing it back out of his eyes.

I held up the paper to show him.

56

"Pass it through and let me see."

I rolled the paper into a long tube and pushed it into the fence. The kid walked up, took the paper, and carefully looked it over. He double-checked it.

"Looks okay," he said, "You'd be surprised how many people try to scam their cars back."

He pulled a ring of keys that was hooked to his belt and, opening the padlock, unwrapped the chain around the two fence gates. With a nod of his head he motioned me inside. I turned to my dad and held a finger up, letting him know I'd be a few minutes, and then stepped in and waited for Andy to replace the chain and lock the gates closed again.

"Can't let nobody in unless I check 'em out first and make sure they got proper papers. Insurance company says so," he explained.

I knew there was more to it than that. Most private companies can't exist on a single government contract. They would have a call service for repair shops as well as several deals with private businesses and shopping malls. That was their bread and butter. Everyone has seen those signs in private parking lots, "No unauthorized parking. Cars will be towed at owner's expense." And those tow companies would hold your car hostage until you came up with the ransom, usually several hundred dollars worth. That's why they had the lock and chain and used them. People get agitated when you tell them it'll cost them three hundred bucks to get their car back all because they parked in the donut shop's lot while they had a few drinks at the bar across the street. Generally, most will try to steal it back if they could.

A few minutes later, after Andy had retrieved the keys from inside his shack, we were standing next to Josie's Infinity. I did a walk around the car, checking it for damage. All I could see was the broken passenger's side window. The interior was clean, except for the broken glass, and a well-worn backpack on the floor of the rear compartment. The backpack was empty except for a few odd scraps of paper, pencils and pens, just like Detective King had said. A quick scan of the rest of the car told me nothing. I would search it thoroughly once I had it back at Josie's house but for now everything seemed as it should.

Andy had me sign another release and, after he had unchained the front gate for me, I pulled Josie's car next to my dad. I yelled across the car through the broken window that I'd meet him back at Josie's house and took off that way. Fifteen minutes later I was crossing the North Bridge again thinking about Josie, her nephew who, like hundreds of other victims, I never met while they were alive, and a

Medical Examiner's Assistant I was supposed to meet in a few hours.

CHAPTER NINE

The campus of Middle South Florida University was situated just north of University Parkway on the west side of Tamiami Trail, across from the airport. It was a small campus area-wise, only a few square blocks, but contained numerous small buildings that housed the classrooms, lecture halls, and administrative offices of the school. There were no dorms or on-campus housing. MSF was a 'commuter campus' that served the local community. Although it started out years ago as a small private university its reputation and standing in the academic community had grown and it was now a very well respected institution. It's innovative degree programs and on-line 'computer commuting' programs were on the cutting edge of upper level education in the southeastern United States.

This expanded reputation and on-line presence made it easy for Leon to research class schedules and download a map of the campus. He had arrived twenty minutes before the class was to begin, which gave him time to scope out the classroom. He parked in a lot just off the main entrance that seemed reserved for visitors and backed into a spot close to the exit. He checked his map and made the short walk to the building.

The class he was interested in was located in a moderately sized brown brick building and was in one of two lecture halls in the building. The lecture halls were on opposite sides of a long corridor that led from the entrance to the back of the building. Leon also saw there were numerous smaller classrooms and offices down several hallways that ran perpendicular to the main corridor at the back of the building. The lecture hall Leon was interested in was on the left side of the corridor and was a fairly large room. It had tiered, stadium-styled seating going downward from the back entrance to a dais at the front of the room. It was big enough where Leon probably wouldn't be noticed in the back of the room. But he wanted to watch the students as they entered.

He picked a spot underneath a tall overhang of another building across the wide concrete pathway so that he was in a deep shadow. He didn't think he would attract much attention on a busy campus, but he didn't want to take the chance someone mistook him for a stalker or other such nutcase. That was why he also wore his uniform. He wasn't sure how well it matched the campus police but it had to be near enough no one should give him a second look, or so he hoped.

He figured it would be easy recognizing the girlfriend; the kid had a bunch of pictures on his cellphone. The other one, the guy, would be harder. He got a description from the kid, Jerry, but it sounded like the description any other school-aged kid these days. Of course, their teacher, this Canby guy would be easy. He'd be the older guy standing in front of the class.

Thinking harder on them now, Leon saw that it was likely the guy and Jerry's girlfriend would enter the classroom from the entrance he was watching. He saw it as the only entrance meant for students. However, it was unlikely Canby would enter the same way. Leon figured most professors and college-level teachers would try to maintain that imaginary line between them and the students and use a private entrance if one were available.

And that was what Leon got stuck on. Was there another entrance for the instructors and teachers? If there was, where was it? Was Canby inside already, in one of the offices preparing for the class, or was he coming from somewhere else? He didn't want to leave his perch and miss the girlfriend and what's-his-name.

Certainly, if Canby were already inside, Leon would not get a look at him from his present spot. Nor would he see him if he used another entrance on the side or rear of the building. But then again, would he need to? He could just wait until the class started and take a look inside. After all, this was just a scouting mission, recon to familiarize him with the other players.

Although there was a need to resolve the problem quickly, Leon knew he had to proceed carefully and not exacerbate the situation. Maybe Jerry wasn't entirely truthful. Even with pharmaceutical assistance Jerry may have lied, or not told everything he knew. Leon had to be sure in order to pull the roots out with the weed.

Leon glanced at his wristwatch, a cheap drugstore digital with a black plastic strap, and saw it was almost time for the class to begin. Several students, boys and girls, had gone into the building and even more had passed by on their way someplace else. The girlfriend, Lindsey was her name Leon remembered, wasn't one of them. The other kid, Joe or Joel was his name, he couldn't be sure. He thought maybe Lindsey and he would be walking together, if he were lucky.

Leon kept his head on a swivel, first eyeing the entrance doors and then each direction along the walkway and back again. Experience told him if he stared too long at a single point the mind would get lazy and wander. His gazed would become fixed and unfocused, almost like a state of hypnosis. He would be as blind as if his eyes were closed.

The pathway was getting crowded with people. Students hurrying as class time drew nearer, others ambling by casually in no hurry at all. Groups of two or three chatting as they walked, single students trotting along, others walking with eyes fixed on cellphones as they thumbed the keyboards. Leon picked her out thirty or forty feet from the entrance. There was no mistaking her, a real cutie with brown hair and high cheekbones. She looked exactly like the pictures on Jerry's phone, except she wasn't smiling.

She was alone. That might make picking out the other kid a little harder. He watched her move down the path and into the building. She walked with purpose, not hurrying but with an objective. Her eyes were fixed straight ahead and not wandering around or on her feet. He trotted across the path and hurried through the entrance. There was no sense staying outside, he didn't know what the other kid looked like yet. Maybe she'd sit next to him. But that wouldn't do any good, he still wouldn't know if that were the guy or not. So, how was he going to solve this problem?

He got inside just in time to see her going into the classroom. He peeked inside and watched her take a seat near the front of the room. There were several others in the classroom already and none acknowledged Lindsey. There were no head nods or hellos or waves directed at Lindsey and she ignored the others as well.

As Leon stood in the hall, holding the door open, several more students bustled by him into the class. He watched each boy, ignoring the girls, and tried to guess which might be the other kid. He noticed most of the girls thanked him for holding the door while the boys either ignored him or gave him a "what are you doing here?" look.

He was about to give up and come back at the end of the class to try again when he saw a kid, a skinny pimple-faced kid, walk up to Lindsey. Their conversation went beyond the casual and quickly got animated, although Leon could see they meant to keep it private. They talked heads close together, obviously whispering, and speaking quickly. Leon was no expert lip reader but he thought he saw Lindsey mouth the names 'Jerry' and 'Joel'.

Leon saw a flash of anger in Lindsey's eyes at something the kid said to her when two other students got close and they ended their conversation. Memorizing the face of the kid talking to Lindsey, Leon was satisfied he had now pegged two out of the three. Canby was the only one he had not yet put eyes on but he would be easy to make.

He checked his wristwatch once again and mentally marked the time to be back as the class got out. Stepping out of the building he decided to walk the campus and get the lay of the land. He was particularly interested in any parking lots the faculty and students might use. It would be important to know it any of the three had cars or used public transportation. Plus, parking garages were great for all sorts of activities being both dark and private. He himself had parked in an employee's lot at the front, or east end, of the property. He was surprised how easy it was to get onto the campus. No one had stopped him or questioned his presence at all.

He started his walk westward, deeper into the meat of the property, following a concrete path. It seemed to be laid out in no particular order with buildings dropped haphazardly here and there. He saw that there was a single road that ran east to west through the property along the north perimeter. Several minor service roads and walkways split off from the road and seemed to snake past some of the buildings and around again back to the road.

Much of the campus was grass and trees and was park-like with benches and common-areas dotted about here and there. To Leon's surprise, the property extended to the Gulf. Planted there, on hundreds of feet of shoreline and what was probably a monstrously valuable piece of real estate, was a large multi-storied building that housed the student union and administrative offices.

He walked around the pink stucco building and along the shore and then again to the footpath. He checked the time and decided to head back to the front of the campus, paying particular attention to the parking lots and garages. He found plenty of ground level lots but no parking structures. Too bad, he thought.

He got back to the classroom before it had let out so he again took a peek inside. And there he was, Mr. Douglas Canby at the head of the class, looking like every other rumpled, shaggy college professor in the world. Or at least, it most likely was he.

Leon closed the door and, as if by plan, a buzzer rang somewhere in the building and students began pouring into the hallway.   He joined the stream and headed outside, taking his old position across the way to wait.

He scanned the faces of the flood of people pushing through the door and rushing in all directions but there were too many of them. He couldn't be sure if Lindsey and the kid Joe had left and he had missed them. The crowd thinned after a few minutes and he was frustrated. He had let an opportunity slip by. He should have been more careful and had a better plan. He didn't want to do this more than he needed to. The more time he spent on the campus increased the odds of him being noticed and confronted.

He was already pulling his car keys from his pocket, giving up for the day, when Lindsey came through the door, head up and marching full steam ahead.

Leon bolted over to her, catching up quickly. Falling in next to her he said, "Police, miss. I need to talk with you."

CHAPTER TEN

Dad pulled in behind me at Josie's house as I was getting out of her car. I told him I needed his car and I wouldn't be back until later tonight.

"What's up? Where you going?" he said.

"I thought I told you earlier, I'm meeting the ME assistant. She's going to let me know the results of the autopsy."

"No, you never said anything about that. You just said we'd find out later."

"I think I did. You probably weren't listening."

"I listened just fine. You never said you were meeting anyone tonight."

"Is it a problem? Do you need the car? I'll just call a cab."

"No, take the friggin' car, I don't need it. I'm just saying you never said nothing about meeting anyone."

"Let's not do this again, okay?"

"Do what? You never said nothing."

"Okay, I never said anything. I thought I did. Let's move on."

"I'm just saying."

"Yeah, I know. So how about the keys then?"

Dad tossed his ring at me and I handed him Josie's keys.

"I want to go through the car real well later, so if you can avoid…"

"Yeah, we'll stay out of it. I'll make her something for dinner or order out or something. We'll figure it out."

"And I might be back late."

"Don't worry about it. Just go home, I'll sleep here. Josie's got plenty of room. I'll call you in the morning."

"Great, that'll work."

We stood there for a moment, both of us looking everywhere except at one another. Dad spoke first.

"So, this ME person is a girl, huh?"

"Yes, a girl, a woman. She's the ME's assistant."

"She good looking?"

"Yes."

"And you asked her out to discuss the case?"

"She asked me out."

"Yeah? Good for you."

And that was the way the Laska men could set each other off and how they apologized to one another.

She didn't like it. This isn't how it's done, she thought. If they wanted to see you they would send a note, a message, usually delivered through a school email account. She stopped anyway, he surprised her and he looked official; a uniform with patches and a badge. He said something about her car and parking violations – lots of them – and that didn't make sense. He must have the wrong person. But he used her name. He took her by the arm and started walking with her, leading her to the parking lots. He smelled sour, like beer and body odor. She didn't like it, this isn't right.

Lindsey tried to pull away but his grip was too strong. He was talking quickly, lecturing her, about paying parking fines on time and penalties for ignoring the notices. She could be suspended, expelled even. But what he was saying didn't make sense. Lindsey never got a parking ticket on campus. She paid an additional fee for a parking spot and had a university-issued sticker affixed to the rear window of her Chevy.

She didn't like it, something was wrong. He was leading her to the East lot not the North lot where she had parked. And why go to the lot? Why not to the

Administration building, or the Campus Police offices, or the Bursar's Office to pay the fines?

He was sweating. He head spun around as he talked, back and forth, back and forth, his eyes looking everywhere. She looked around and saw no one. No students, no teachers, no maintenance workers. It was like everyone else had evaporated. She stopped walking. This was wrong. She can't go with him.

His momentum carried him forward and jerked her arm as he stopped and spun to face her. He still had a grip on her arm, she was shaking and her mouth was dry. Her backpack, gripped by her other hand, hung to the ground.

"You're not Campus Police," she said fighting her fear.

He tightened his grip. She tried to pull away but he yanked her closer and started walking again, pulling her along.

"Lindsey!"

She heard it, her name being called somewhere behind her. She tried to stop again, her feet stumbling forward as he kept walking.

"Lindsey!"

Again, getting closer. It was Joel, trotting towards them.

He tried moving her along faster but she pulled back harder, her arm and shoulder was aching. She dug her feet in, arching her back and used her legs for leverage. It worked and he jerked to a stop. He turned and stared at her with bloodshot eyes. He looked over her shoulder towards Joel and unclamped his hand from her arm. He walked away without a word.

Joel caught up. "What was that? Who was that cop, what did he want?"

"We're in trouble. I really have to find Jerry."

CHAPTER ELEVEN

Leon kept his head on a swivel and hurried to his car. He didn't run, that might attract more attention, but he moved quickly. He saw no one. No one followed him and even the occasional pedestrian he saw paid no attention to him. He slowed down, no sense in hurrying now.

He reached his car, fired it up, and turned up the air conditioning. It wasn't that warm out but he was sweating like a priest at an Altar Boy convention. He wiped his brow with the back of his hand and dried it in his armpit.

That didn't go well, he thought. But that was his fault for not planning better. This was only supposed to be a scouting mission but when he saw that bitch Lindsey walk off alone he thought he could take advantage. He thought he had her. She was confused and intimidated. He was leading her and she was following. But she caught on. Leon thought that wouldn't have mattered by that point. They were close to the lot he had parked in and he certainly could have over-powered her, put her in the trunk and that would have been that.

But the other kid saw them, saw Leon and Lindsey, and butted in. Leon couldn't take the chance. If the girl yelled out for help, would the kid run off and call the police or would he confront Leon and force a physical altercation? An altercation Leon was absolutely sure he would win but that wouldn't matter. A fight, more like a beating, out in the open was too risky. Or would he just follow them to Leon's car and maybe get his license plate? Leon couldn't chance any of those so he let Lindsey go.

Now she knew something was up and she knew his face. Getting to her would be more difficult. The other kid might be easier, he probably didn't get a good look at Leon, but Leon couldn't be sure of that either. Anyway, they would all be wired up now. Even that teacher, Canby. They'd be extra cautious and maybe even call the police. And then again, maybe not. Calling the police would mean admitting to a crime. It would be a conspiracy, a conspiracy to commit a burglary, or breaking and entering at least.

He was cooling down. The A/C vents were aimed straight at his face. He was trying to figure out what his next move was, how he was going to get close enough in a secluded area. He would probably have to track them to their homes. He might have to do it there.

Leon was grinding away on his problem. His head started to hurt, it could have been a brain-freeze from the A/C, when Douglas Canby walked right in front of Leon's 1991 Chevy Camaro IROC Z28.

Leon was surprised but he didn't hesitate, better sooner than later he reasoned. He put his car in gear. He crept out of the spot and turned towards Canby who was walking down the center of the aisle, his back to Leon.

Pulling out his best NASCAR moves, Leon depressed the clutch, slammed the accelerator to the floor, and released the clutch. The IROC leapt forward, tires squealing, with a cloud of smoke spewing from the tires and exhaust. Leon corrected a minor fishtail as the tires grabbed the asphalt. He pointed the center of the hood at Douglas Canby who was just becoming aware of the sounds of the hurtling mass of metal coming towards him.

When it was new, the Chevy Camaro IROC Z28 with its 5.0-liter, 230 horsepower V8 could go from a dead stop to sixty miles an hour in about six and a half seconds. It would cover the distance of a quarter mile in fifteen seconds. But that was over 20 years and three owners ago. And Leon had neither the financial resources nor the ambition to keep his auto in peak condition. It was transportation to him. One he erroneously thought was stylish but still only transportation.

Douglas Canby was no more than seventy feet from the IROC when it began its race towards him. He whipped his head around at the sound. He jumped aside between two parked cars as Leon slammed on the brakes and swerved. Leon was unable to gain control and struck one of the cars near Canby, breaking his headlight and crumpling his fender. The other car fared no better suffering a broken taillight and dented side panel.

"What the hell is going on? You almost hit me," Canby said.

"Shut up, asshole," Leon said jumping from the IROC. He grabbed the surprised Canby by his collar. Leon pulled him towards his car.

"What is this, let go of me!" he said pulling away.

Leon needed to get Canby into his car quickly. Someone could walk through at anytime. He spun around and punched Canby full in the face. Blood gushed from his nose and his eyes rolled back in his head. He fell straight back, his head taking the full impact of the pavement.

Leon stood over Canby. He couldn't tell if he was breathing. He grabbed Canby by the ankles and pulled him from between the cars. He got back into his car and rolled over Canby's head.

As the car rolled over him, Canby's body became wedged underneath and was dragged until Leon stopped the car. Leon opened his door, poked his head under the car, and cursed his luck. It took three attempts rocking the vehicle back and forth before Leon freed the Camaro from the mangled body of Douglas Canby. He pulled out of the lot, onto Tamiami Trail and drove home, stopping for a six-pack on the way.

CHAPTER TWELVE

After showering and shaving I dressed in the cleanest knit golf shirt I could find, a pair of khaki shorts, and well-worn sandals. For Florida, in early May, that was as dressy as anyone gets. I took the North Bridge to the mainland again and then north on Osprey to Tamiami Trail. I passed the Marina and Island Park on the left and the adjacent parking lot where, according to Detective Nosmo King, Jerry's body had been found.

A few minutes later I was turning right onto First Avenue. I saw the restaurant halfway down the block. A sign in front said they had free valet service but it never really is. You've got to tip the kid or feel like an ass, or a snowbird. I was having cash flow problems since I stopped working so I found a spot down the street and wedged the Cadillac into it.

Inside, at the hostess station, I asked for the rooftop bar and was directed to an elevator nearby. The building was an old warehouse of some kind; stripped down to walls of sandblasted brick, bare wood beams and black steel girders. Colorful Spanish-style tile covered the dark oak tables. Wrought iron twisted into curly-cue shapes framed the staircase and partitioned the space into several rooms. It was all very trendy.

The elevator was a new addition, or maybe it had replaced an old steel cage lift to meet the building code. I stepped off on the roof and was splashed by the sun in the western sky. I shaded my eyes with a hand and did a quick scan. Directly in front of me was a long bar, cheaply built with thick lumber green with chemical preservatives and insecticides. To the left of me and in front of the bar was a large space filled with tables and chairs made of the same lumber, weathering grey from the sun and rain. A canvas canopy covered the bar and half of the roof offering some shade to the fair skinned or those who forgot their sunglasses.

I spotted Gabrielle Jones sitting on the far, sunny side of the roof. She was seated on a barstool at a bistro table facing the sun. She wore a rather tight-fitting pale blue sundress and pink flip-flops with toenails painted to match. Her eyes were closed and her face was tilted up into the light. Her hands were folded on her lap and her whole body leaned slightly forward as if she were inviting in the sunlight. The light from the setting sun gave her skin a rosy glow and surrounded her like a halo.

I almost hated to intrude, but I did.

"Hi," I said, pulling out the barstool opposite her, "You look so peaceful."

"Well, you've got to grab those little bits when you can." She smiled wide and opened her eyes. They were green.

"Sorry I'm late," I said.

"I only got here a few minutes ago myself," she said. "I had to work late, a traffic accident victim."

I sat and smiled back. It was a genuine smile. Just sitting with her made me feel good, and I didn't even know her yet.

"Of course I came. I may have been a little slow on the uptake this morning but I'm not stupid. Or at least I like to think I'm not."

"I'm glad, Sam Laska."

"Just Sam. And so, what do I call you? Your nametag said 'Gabrielle Jones'. Do you like Gabrielle or Gabby or maybe just Jones?"

"Marley. I've always been Marley. It's my middle name. I only use Gabrielle for official stuff. And God! Never Gabby."

"Got it, never Gabby. So, Marley? Like Bob Marley?"

"Yeah, I guess. It's spelled the same way. But I wasn't named after him." She hitched her chair in a little closer and let out a small sigh almost like she was tired of explaining but she was still smiling so I let her continue. "My mother loved the Beatles and especially 'Ob-la-di, Ob-la-da'. You know, the song? Well, in the lyrics the husband and wife are named Desmond and Molly, right?"

"If you say so."

"My mother thinks the wife's name is Marley, 'cause you know, that's what it sounded like to her. My dad was Jamaican and she loved him so much and thought it would make him happy so she gave me a middle name that she thought was Jamaican."

"That's sweet. So why not just name you Marley? Is Gabrielle a family name or something?"

"No, my mom was a pretty devout Christian, lots of Seminoles are. Gabrielle is supposed to mean 'God is my strength' in Hebrew. That stuff was important to her so Gabrielle had to be my first name."

The waitress came and I was happy for it. I was thirsty and I hadn't eaten all day.

Marley pointed to an empty glass half full of fruit in front of her and asked for another sangria. I ordered a light beer. Marley asked to see a menu and the waitress was off.

"We'll eat here, okay? It's too nice out here to go inside."

"Sure," I said, "What's good here? What kind of food do they serve? Spanish I'm guessing."

"Yeah, tapas. It's great. Have you ever had it before?"

"No, I don't think so. It's some kind of fish, isn't it?"

She laughed at that but quickly realized I wasn't kidding. "No. It means small plates of food, fish, meats, cheeses, and stuff. It's kind of like appetizers. We'll order a bunch and share. You'll try all kinds of different things. You're gonna love it."

I said okay and smiled, but I was pretty sure I was going to go home hungry.

The waitress came back with our drinks and menus and Marley ordered for us both. We made more small talk until the food came. When it did, Marley took charge, explaining to me what each dish was and even put the first few things on my plate.

We talked as we ate, getting to know each other better. "So you're Seminole and Jamaican. How did your parents meet?" I said.

"In the sugar cane fields down south in the 'Glades, near West Palm Beach. My dad's family came over when he was a boy and the whole family worked in the fields. My mom's family lived in the area. They came north from the Big Cypress reservation. They actually met at church and fell in love. The mixed race thing was frowned on and their families tried to keep them apart but young love prevailed. They ran away, eloped, when they were old enough. They saved some money and bought a small piece of land near Arcadia. That's where I was born and grew up."

"Arcadia," I said. "It seems every exit sign on I-75 from Tampa to Fort Myers points the way to Arcadia. All roads in Florida lead to Arcadia, I guess."

"I know what you mean. The good thing is that those same roads lead *out* of Arcadia. And after my parents died I followed the first one out as soon as I could. My uncle helped me get my job and here I am."

"I'm sorry."

"Why? I'm sure not. I couldn't wait to get out of that place."

"No, I mean I'm sorry about your parents."

84

She stopped halfway to her mouth with a forkful of some kind of saucy-meaty thing. Putting the fork down on her plate she sighed again, remembering. "My mom died suddenly when I was eleven. One day she was healthy, the next she was in bed, coughing and spitting up blood. She died the same night. We never found out what it was. My dad, I found in the field out back of the house. We had a big garden where we grew tomatoes, lettuce, beans, and all kinds of stuff. We lived off that garden and sold what we couldn't eat or can for ourselves. The doctor called it a heart attack. That was two years ago.

It was hard growing up without my mom. You know, girl stuff, puberty. I have an uncle and aunt here in Sarasota and my aunt would visit often and the neighborhood ladies would help out too. My dad did a good job. He loved me so much. After he died I gave up the house and land and came here to Sarasota. Kind of a fresh start."

"I'm sorry. I'm sorry you had it so tough."

"Thanks." She picked up her forkful and said, "And what about you?" she said, her mood picking up. "Tell me about yourself. Why did you retire? Why move to Florida? Chicago must be a great city. It must be big, huh? Busy and exciting?"

"It's not as great as you might think; the traffic, the weather, the crime, the politics. You forget about the great theater, restaurants, sports, and all the other stuff. You can get real soured on it. At least when you live there you forget how good it can be. I like it here. This is home now."

"Spoken like a cop. But you must miss some things about it."

"Sure. Like I said, the restaurants are unbeatable, it's got one of the best theater scenes in the country, and there's nothing like the lakefront in the summer."

"Have you been to Siesta Key's beach yet?"

"Yeah, I know. But, well, it's different back home. It's got a certain vibe, a living, breathing feel to it. Here it's like the dawn of the nearly dead. The old folks are marching back and forth, up and down the beach like zombies. The beach is beautiful here, but the feel is different."

"You know, you just called Chicago home. You said 'back home'."

"Habit I guess. I'll probably always think of it as home, always be a Cubs and Bears fan, but I live here now. And I'm not kidding, I like it."

"It's easy to fall in love with this place. But you obviously still like Chicago, no matter what you say. Why did you leave? Why did a young guy like you quit his job and move to Florida."

I drained the last swallow of my beer, held the bottle up, and gave a nod to the waitress. I never really talked about this with anyone. My dad knew, other people back on the job knew, but I never talked to anyone about it. Since I left it never occurred to me that I might have to.

"First, I'm not as young as you probably think. I'm forty-three." Marley scrunched her lips up and nodded her head like she thought that was still okay. "Second, I know there's not a lot of difference but I retired, I didn't quit. I was vested, had my twenty years in, but not the age. I'll get a pension, a teeny-tiny pension, when I hit fifty and not a penny until then. But all that is a technicality. I was forced off. I was given the choice to retire or be fired."

Marley was sitting back in her chair now, glass in hand, and listening closely. Fired or retired, it was all the same to me. But getting fired stigmatizes you. No matter how unjust it may have been people will always doubt your story. They'll figure any defense is sour grapes on your part and wonder what the truth is, why you were really forced off.

"So what happened?" she said.

"It's embarrassing. I don't want you to get the wrong impression of me."

87

"If you don't tell me, I'll just make something up which will probably be worse than what really happened."

I thought about it. "Okay, you win. I'll roll the dice." I leaned in closer to her. I didn't want anyone to overhear what I was going to say. "It was last July, I was assigned as lead detective on a shooting in a nightclub. Three dead, eight wounded. At least five people had guns. It was a gang shoot-out. The club had security guards working the door and everyone got searched going in. But it was common knowledge you could skip the search for twenty bucks. At one in the morning the place turned into the OK Corral. Ironic thing was one of the dead victims was a security guard."

"We had a ton of reluctant witnesses, including the surviving shooting victims and a handful of suspects. One of them was a leader of one of the involved gangs. We transport him back to our office and put him in a secured interview room. I tell the transport car to watch him because I'm going to order a GSR, a gunshot residue test, to see if he fired a gun."

Marley spoke. "I bet I know what's coming."

"I get back to the station and the transport guys are drinking coffee, laughing and joking across the room. I check on my prisoner and, guess what?"

"He's licking his hands clean, beating the test."

"You're on the right track. He's peeing on them. He's actually washing his hands in his own urine. The asshole cops told him he was going to be GSR'd and he pissed on his own hands."

Marley's eyes went wide and then she started laughing. I almost did too.

"I would have gone with licking my hands clean," she said.

"Go ahead and laugh now," I said, "It gets ugly from here." The waitress brought my beer and I took a big swig. "When I saw that I lost it. A triple homicide, eight more shot, and one of my main suspects is destroying evidence. I grab him and spin him around, pulling his hands away. Naturally, as I spin him, he pees all over my pants and shoes. I haul back and punch him. He falls back and hits his head on the concrete wall and goes down, out like a light. He gets concussed, spends two weeks in the hospital, and nearly dies.

The Public Defender is outraged. At least he acts like it, and demands my head. The City wants to cut their losses. They see the lawsuit on the horizon. I'm sent to the Department shrink. His evaluation said I have chronic anger management issues. I'm told to retire or get fired."

Marley was shaking her head. "One mistake and they hammer you like that?"

"That was the climate. There had been a few other scandals that broke in the papers and there was a zero tolerance policy." I didn't tell her I also had several prior beefs that landed me in hot water.

I felt my blood pressure rising and my jaw tightening, like it did nearly a year ago. I hoped Marley didn't notice. I took another sip of my beer. I sat back and took a deep breath. I tried to remember the tricks the shrink taught me.

"And you know what the worst part is? I wasn't really angry with the suspect. He was just doing what he had to do and I was taking it out on him. It was those two asshole coppers who did the transport I should have punched. They told the suspect he was going to get GSR'd, they un-cuff him, and don't watch him. They wind up getting a formal reprimand for Inattention to Duty and I get fired."

"You retired."

"Yeah, but it sure feels like I got fired." I put my beer down and let out a sigh. "So?" I said, "The Department shrink says I have a bad temper. Maybe I do, I don't know. But you see why I was reluctant to talk about it. It's not typical conversation for a first date and I didn't want to scare you off."

"Yeah, I understand. Listen, we're still getting to know each other and we're going to see where that leads. So far it sounds like you had something to be angry about. And I'm still here, aren't I?" She smiled and leaned in closer to me.

I smiled back. "I'm glad."

CHAPTER THIRTEEN

We had another drink and Marley ordered another round of tapas. Dried sausage and cheese, salty and sweet olives, smoked mussels, and something called Baba Ganoush I only tasted to make Marley happy. We talked about her job and my lack of one. I told her I was getting by on my rapidly dwindling savings by giving up my car and apartment in Chicago and moving in with my dad. I tried to explain my father and our relationship but family things are never understood well by outsiders.

"My dad is a piece of work, a little guy with the classic Napoleon complex. He retired from the police department too. He's opinionated, bigoted, egotistical, and selfish. We don't often see eye to eye."

"You said you're living with him?"

"Yeah, we try to stay out of each other's way."

"But he invited you into his home when you needed help, put you up, doesn't ask for rent I expect?"

"True."

"Maybe you need to lighten up on him a little."

"Maybe, and maybe you should meet him before you decide I'm too hard on him." I smiled and she smiled back.

"Fair enough."

We talked about her plans. She wanted to go back to school but really didn't have any idea what she wanted to do or study.

"I just don't know," she said. "All I know for sure is I don't want to spend my life in the morgue. It's a dead end, pun intended. What about you? Are you going to keep freeloading or find honest work?"

"It's not so easy for me. I'm an ex-cop with a degree in Criminal Justice. What can I do? I'm too old to start back again with a sheriff's department or police department down here. Plus, if I've got nothing when that lawsuit comes knocking, they can't take anything."

"That's just an excuse."

"Yep, but I'm enjoying not working," I lied. "Maybe retirement won't be so bad."

She gave me a 'we'll see' look, another smile, and changed the subject.

"So anyway, Dr. Cortez posted your friend's grandson."

"And?"

"And it's like we thought, probably an OD. We sent blood, urine, and tissue samples off to the lab for the tox screen."

"Nothing unusual then? It is what it is?"

"Not quite. Like we talked about, it appears the drugs were orally ingested. Funny thing is there were two partially dissolved pills in his stomach. That's way too much. Also, since they were only partially dissolved, he had to have already ingested enough to kill him and then took two more pills."

"That doesn't sound right."

"Unless he was trying to kill himself. And that doesn't make sense, right? No note was found and kids that age always leave notes. Am I right?"

"Typically, but not always. There would be some obvious signs, though. Like trouble with a girlfriend, or pressures at school, or maybe a fight with his grandmother."

"Any of those things happen?"

"His grandmother said things were good lately, as far as she knew. I haven't talked to the girlfriend yet. His grandmother said there was one but I haven't looked for her yet."

"There's something else. There's perimortem trauma to the inside of his right elbow and both wrists."

"What kind of trauma?"

"That's difficult to say. The trauma to the elbow is more pronounced and was probably sustained about an hour before death. The trauma to the wrists is less pronounced and more difficult to get a handle on."

"Think it could have been caused by restraints of some kind?"

"Dr. Cortez won't commit to that. I asked him too. All he'll say is it 'appears' there is some trauma there but he can't be sure. His preliminary ruling is accidental death due to acute intoxication by oxycodone."

"Did you tell this to Detective King yet?"

"He'll get the report in the morning."

"And he'll see there's no reason not to close it out as an accidental OD."

"Are you sure?"

"If I were him I'd do the same."

"But?"

"But my antennae are quivering a little. There's enough for me to keep looking at it."

"Are you going to tell King?"

"Hell no. He would tell me to stay away and he would be completely right."

With that we turned our attention back to each other. We lingered over our last drinks, moving closer to one another, flirting, telling cute and funny stories from our jobs and our lives until the lights were clicked off, the bartender began a cleanup routine, and our waitress put the check down on the table.

Marley tried to grab it but I was faster. She invited me out, she protested. I paid with a credit card and was relieved when it came back approved.

Downstairs, I got the door while she dug a valet ticket out of a small beaded purse. While we waited for her car I told her I'd like to see her again.

"Well, let me think," she said. "You're taller than me, and tall enough that I can wear heels, you've got pretty blue eyes, a nice butt, and you've got all your hair. You paid for dinner even though you're broke. You passed the honesty test, you held the door for me, you've got a good sense of humor and we have lots in common. We also have enough differences to make it interesting. I'd say we definitely have potential." And then, putting on a lilting Jamaican accent, she said, "Sam Laska, Ahm tinkin we's mi' be good fer wan anotter."

Marley kissed me as the valet pulled up in a beat up 1970's era Ford pickup that had seen a long life of hard farm labor. The kiss was longer than a first kiss should be yet shorter than I wanted it to be. She climbed into the truck and the old door creaked loudly as I pushed it closed.

She smiled again and she was gone. As she drove away I said to myself, "I never got her phone number."

CHAPTER FOURTEEN

I was right. I was still hungry. I tried to think of somewhere to get a quick burger that wasn't McDonald's. It was late by Sarasota standards. At eleven o'clock most places downtown were already closed. The Hob Nob was sure to be shut down for the night too. I remembered there were a few places in the Gulf Gate neighborhood not far from the south bridge to Siesta Key that kept late hours. I got in the Caddy and headed that way.

I took the Trail south again. I could have taken Main Street east to Washington and south again to pick up the Trail after it snaked the long way around downtown. Instead, I backtracked the same way I came. It was a little longer but it took me past the marina. I was on the section of Tamiami Trail renamed Bayfront Drive by the City. It followed the shoreline and passed the marina and the adjacent Island Park. It reminded me of a shorter version of Lake Shore Drive in Chicago. Before I ate I wanted to see where Jerry was found.

I turned right onto Ringling Boulevard, which intersected Bayfront Drive and rolled into the entrance of the marina's parking lot. I turned left onto Island Park Drive, a service drive that was part street and part parking lot, and crept slowly south.

Descriptions and pictures of crime scenes are fine for show-and-tell with judges and juries. And they're necessary to memorialize the scene and capture the important items and their relationship to one another. But nothing replaces being there. The details and subtle nuances of the exact scene and the surrounding area, the angles of sight from various locations a witness may have been standing, the litter and debris on the ground, the smells and the atmosphere can't all be captured by a camera. You had to go there, be there, see, feel, hear, and smell it for yourself. It was best to be on a scene immediately after it was found but I couldn't do that. This was next best.

I drove slowly along the drive towards the far south end where Jerry was found in Josie's car. The lot also mimicked the curve of the Trail and narrowed as it was squeezed between the street and the shoreline. It was a fairly secluded location far from the main parking area.

It was dark, the closest street lamp was at least fifty yards away, and it was framed by clumps of foliage that created darker patches of shadow and kept the headlamps of passing cars from illuminating the area.

The lights of the Caddy picked up the glint of broken glass on the pavement ahead. Tiny pebbles of tempered auto glass, about half of a side windows worth, marked the spot for me. I stopped the car, got out and stood next to the small mound. I glanced around and quickly came to the conclusion there was not going to be much in the way of evidence to be found. Matching the glass on the ground to Josie's car wasn't necessary and it could barely even be called evidence. The asphalt pavement wouldn't yield any footprints and the breeze off the bay made sure I wouldn't find other trace evidence. I could see no signs of security cameras anywhere nearby. At least I now understood the seclusion of the area. It was perfect for anyone who needed shadowy privacy.

I walked towards the water. I crossed a narrow ribbon of grass that sloped down to another of sand that stopped at the edge of the water. The night was clear and from the light of a half moon and its reflection off the bay, I could see the shoreline. It was littered with several rotting dinghies and abandoned rowboats. Some were probably still used to shuttle boaters to the yachts and sailboats in the marina but most looked like tiny shipwrecks. I walked north along the water's edge following the curve of the bay and weaving around the occasional decaying vessel.

I found what I was looking for fairly soon and fairly close. Piled inside a dented aluminum rowboat was a mass of rags wrapped around a thin, sunburned, hairy being that smelled of sour sweat, mildewed cloth, cigarette smoke, and salt. He was curled up on his side, his right hand under his head for a pillow, but he wasn't asleep. His eyes were open and staring at me.

"How're you doing," I said, "Nice night, huh?"

"This your boat?" he asked me. He turned and sat upright.

"No. Are you around here everyday? Do you sleep here?"

"You a cop?"

"Nope."

"You ask questions like a cop." He settled back down on his side again.

"Trust me, I'm not a cop."

"You got a square?"

"A square? No, sorry, I don't smoke."

"Too bad."

"Can I ask you a few things?"

"One question, one smoke, then one answer," he said.

"I don't have any cigarettes. I'd give you as many as you wanted if I did."

"No cigarettes, no questions, no answers."

"How about I give you a couple of dollars? Then you could go buy some."

"A pack costs eight dollars."

"Fine, I'll give you eight dollars." I pulled out my wallet and started counting through the bills, hoping I had enough for cigarettes and a burger later.

"Closest store is over ten blocks away, the Walgreen's over on Fruitville."

I stopped pulling the bills from my wallet. "You're telling me you want a ride now?"

"I ain't gonna walk. I get the gout now and again. And it's been awhile since I rode in a Cadillac."

I looked back towards Dad's car. It was nestled in the far end of the lot a good fifty yards away near the exact spot Josie's car was found. Even with the moonlight it was dark and deeply shaded by the bushes and a few low growing palms. It was difficult to see if you weren't paying attention.

"You see me pull in?"

"Yep. Watched you pull in from the street way back there." He nodded towards the entrance. "Followed you all the way 'til you parked over there. Watched you get out of the Caddy and kept watching you all the way over to here."

"You've got good eyes. You here every night?"

"Yep."

"Last night?"

"Yep."

"Let's go get you those smokes," I said.

It was a short ride to the Walgreen's, only five minutes or so. I had all the windows rolled down and the fan on full. But his stink was powerful, and I wondered if it would dissipate before I gave Dad his car back. I smiled to myself and secretly hoped it wouldn't. I jumped out to get the cigarettes, remembering to take the keys with me.

"I smoke menthols," he said. "And don't forget matches."

When I got back I handed him the pack and matches. He ripped it open, stuck a smoke in the side of his mouth and lit up. He inhaled deeply and started coughing so badly I thought he would die right there. He hacked up a glob of goo and spit it out the window.

"What's your name?" I said, turning in my seat to face him but trying not to inhale too deeply.

Between more coughing and spitting he told me to call him Captain Bob.

"That your real name?"

"Never met anyone who's real name was Captain."

"I meant Bob. Is Bob your real name?"

"Yeah."

"You got a last name?"

"See, I knew you was a cop. Nobody but a cop would care what my name was."

"I'm not a cop. Really. I used to be, now I'm just an ordinary citizen."

"I guess it don't matter. Either way, I figure you for a good guy."

"Why's that?" I said.

"Bad guy wouldn't be so polite. Bad guy wouldn't bribe me with smokes. Bad guy probably would of threatened me or hit me or something."

"Why would a bad guy be interested in talking to you?"

"Same reason you are."

"Which is?"

"Last night. When that other cop drove in with the dead kid."

"Say that again." I said.

"That's what you wanted to talk to me about, right? When he left the dead kid in the white Infinity."

CHAPTER FIFTEEN

"You're telling me some cop drove a white Infinity into the parking lot, parked, and then left, leaving a dead body in the car."

"Broke the window too, real shame, a nice car like that. People got no respect for nice things any more. Then he made a phone call. Talked only a little while and tossed the phone back in the car and then walked off casual as can be. He went back through the lot to the street and kept walking." He nodded in the direction of Ringling Boulevard.

"You're sure? You're sure it was a cop?"

"You think I don't know what a cop looks like? He was a white guy, dark hair, shorter than you by a head. Not fat but he had a belly. It stuck out good. He had to hitch his pants up a few times, you know, because it was so big. He had a white shirt on, dark jacket over it with some kind of patches on the sleeves. Plain dark pants and cop shoes. Didn't see no gun though."

"The city police wear blue shirts. I think the county wears green," I said. I was sure I remembered seeing some area police officers in white shirts. I wondered if supervisors wore white shirts to distinguish themselves from police officers as they did in Chicago.

"Don't know nothing about shirts. I just know he was a cop."

"You know," I said, "I talked to a detective earlier today. He told me homeless people, street people like you, sometimes break into the cars in the lot. To sleep or steal."

"You saying I broke the window?"

"Maybe not you. Maybe it was one of your friends and you're covering up for him. You're not lying to me, are you?"

"You think I drove the car in too? Maybe killed the kid? I got no reason to lie."

I didn't know what else to say. He could be lying. But to what end? He would have no reason to mislead me. There were details in his story, like the white shirt, that even a practiced liar wouldn't think of adding. If you were going to lie about it why not just say it was a blue shirt like the city cops wear? I worked that over a few times and came to the conclusion he was probably telling me the truth about what he saw. Or, at least what he believed he saw.

"I went over there, by the car," he said. "After he left. I saw the dead kid in the car, in the back seat. I knew he was dead right away. Seen lotsa dead ones. Mostly people like me. When I heard the sirens coming, I went back to my boat to sleep."

"The boy was dead when you saw him. Do you think he may have been alive when the car pulled into the lot?"

"Couldn't say. I only know he was dead when I saw him."

"You saw the police show up too? In squad cars?"

"Yep, lights flashing and everything."

"And you didn't go talk to them, tell them what you saw?"

"Nope, none of my business. Besides, I don't get along with the police. Most of them ain't very nice."

"Didn't they come around, looking for any witnesses, like you?"

"Don't think so. I probably wouldn't have said anything anyway. Like I said, it wasn't none of my business. "

"Then why are you telling me?"

"You bought me cigarettes."

Just that simple. I sat forward in my seat. Bob tossed a butt that was nothing but smoldering filter out the window and lit another. I started up the Caddy.

"Would you recognize that cop again, the one who broke the window?" I said.

Without hesitation Bob answered, "Yep."

I put the car in gear.

"You gonna take me back now, huh? Too bad, these seats are plenty comfortable. Better than that old boat. Don't this leather get hot in the daytime though?"

"I'm not taking you back yet, Bob. You've got to tell the police what you told me. They think the boy in the car died accidentally, an overdose. What you're saying changes that."

"I ain't gonna talk to the police. I told you, I don't get along with them."

"Bob, it won't take long. The police station is only a few blocks away. I promise you they'll be nice to you. As nice as me."

"No. I ain't gonna talk to them. You think I'm going to tell a room full of cops I saw another cop do wrong? You're crazy! You take me there and I'll just shut up. I won't say nothing or I'll tell them I made up the whole thing, so you can just take me back or let me out right here."

I couldn't blame him. I saw real fear in his face and it was convincing. I doubted the person Bob saw was a Sarasota police officer but I wasn't sure, and I knew I had to be before I outed Bob. I couldn't lose him, what he knew was too important. This accidental overdose wasn't accidental.

"Okay, Bob, you win. I'll take you back." I said. And I did.

CHAPTER SIXTEEN

I was up at the crack of nine, early by my current standards, and still hungry. I never got that burger last night. I put a pot of coffee on to brew while I showered, shaved, and dressed. A polo shirt and dress pants today. I wanted to look business casual just in case.

It had been a little less than twenty-four hours since my dad woke me asking for help. A lot had happened since then, but a lot usually happens in the first twenty-four hours of a homicide investigation.

That's what this is, I thought. There was no other explanation I could come up with. I fell asleep last night thinking about it and started right up again when I awoke. The facts were simple. Jerry was driven to the Bayfront and left either dead or dying in his car by a police officer that broke the car's window to stage the crime scene. He called it in and then casually walked off. Two partially dissolved oxycodone pills were found in Jerry's stomach. The amount of oxy his body absorbed from those two pills was unlikely to have killed him. Therefore, he had ingested more prior to that. Again, the only reasonable explanation I could think of is an intentional overdose and not a suicide. The actions of the police officer prove that. And there are unexplained injuries to both wrists that may or may not have been caused by restraints, maybe handcuffs.

When the toxicology report comes back and shows Jerry had overdosed on more than what was found in his stomach and, if I can get Captain Bob to talk, I thought I would have proof enough that Jerry's death was a homicide. The Sarasota Police, specifically Detective Nosmo King, would be forced to open a homicide investigation. How keen would they be on investigating a police officer for murder though? This was a small town and a small police department where every cop knew every other cop, even from the surrounding jurisdictions, of which there were many.

There were the neighboring cities like Bradenton, Venice, and Longboat Key. Then the Sarasota County Sheriff's Department, and Manatee County's Sheriff's Department, and the State Highway Patrol. There were even Police Departments on most of the university campuses in the area. I doubted a conspiracy but you never know. I would need to be careful approaching King again.

I did see some other problems. Captain Bob was not the most reliable witness I'd ever had. I let his refusal to give me a last name slide in order to keep him talking to me. Had I interviewed him in an official capacity that would never have happened. There was a chance his story was a lie or a delusion, but I doubted it. Detective King might not see it that way, though.

Jerry himself was a problem too. What was he doing out at that time of night? Like a murdered prostitute, could he be viewed as being accountable for his own death by virtue of a lifestyle choice or decision? In other words, was he a doper? I needed more than Josie's feelings on that.

I poured myself a cup of coffee, cream and sugar, and fetched the newspaper. I stood at the kitchen counter sipping and scanned the headlines. There was another parking meter scandal brewing in town and the governor was on a statewide tour trying to bring his numbers up before the election. I pushed it aside and refilled my cup.

I would need to clear up some, if not all, of my questions before I brought it to Detective King. I wrote a To Do list in my head and checked the clock on the microwave. Nine-forty. I took my coffee, jumped in the Caddy, and headed over to Josie's house.

Several miles to the south, on Casey Key, Dr. Marko Rutikov was being served his second cup of coffee. Only his wasn't prepared in a twenty-three dollar Mr. Coffee machine with a grocery store grind. Dr. Rutikov was enjoying a latte macchiato prepared by his personal chef using a three thousand dollar Swiss-made, whisper-quiet, Jura Impressa professional model coffee system and fresh ground Jacu Bird coffee from Brazil. He sipped his beverage while nibbling on a warm blueberry scone and enjoying the soft sea breeze coming off the Gulf of Mexico.

Rutikov's home was at the farthest point north on Casey Key, a prime two-acre lot. On the lot he had built the largest and most profane abomination seen this side of Frank Gehry. The architecture was a disagreeable meld of Gothic, Greek, and medieval Romanesque styles. The building was basically a long, three-story box that resembled the result of a horrible sci-fi movie transporter machine accident with the Parthenon and King Arthur's castle that was then dipped in faux stone and pink stucco.

The veranda, paved in Italian marble, stretched the length of the building. Steps led down to a second marble deck with an Infinity pool and ringed by a waist-high carved stone pillared fence. Beyond the fence was the white sand beach of the Gulf of Mexico.

Dr. Rutikov was a wealthy man and enjoyed demonstrating that fact to anyone and everyone. He drove, or rather was driven in, expensive automobiles – he owned three: a Bentley Mulsanne, a Porsche Cayenne, and a fully restored 1968 Shelby Cobra GT 500KR convertible. He wore only the finest clothes, shopped in the best stores, ate in the best restaurants, and was seen at all the right parties. He was a fixture on the Sarasota social scene and was a major contributor and patron of the Ringling museum, the Asolo Theater, the local film festival, and any other charitable organization or function that caught his attention or could get his name in the papers. He was also a major financial supporter of the Governor.

Rutikov perused the newspaper as he ate. He scanned the article that described the travel itinerary of the Governor and wondered how much more it was going to cost him to keep the idiot in Tallahassee. He then turned his attention to the Metro section. On page three, between short articles describing the discovery of a meth lab and the arrest of a purse-snatching suspect, he found what he was looking for.

It was another article, three sentences actually, that told of the discovery of the body of a young man in the parking lot of the marina. A drug overdose was suspected.

The victim's name was withheld pending notification of relatives.

Rutikov was pleased. It appeared his instructions had been followed adequately. He had almost turned the page and closed the section when he saw another story on the opposite page. The bold-lettered lead read *Fatal Hit and Run on MSFU Campus*. The article stated police were seeking any information regarding a hit and run collision in a parking lot on the campus. Killed in the collision was Douglas Canby, a tenured professor of Journalism and one time Pulitzer candidate. A police department's spokesperson stated no information on the involved vehicle was known at this time and any persons with information should contact the police immediately.

Rutikov pulled a cellphone from his pocket and dialed Leon Irsay's number.

"Yeah, Doc," Leon answered. He was slurring his words.

"I told you no other action until we have all the files," Rutikov said.

"Yeah, that wasn't supposed to happen. I tried to grab him but he fought back. It got out of hand. I made it look like an accident though."

"Did you get his files at least?"

"Um, no. But I'm gonna go back for them."

"And how do you know where they are? Do you know if he gave copies to anyone?"

"Um, no but…"

Rutikov punched the end button. He felt a hot flush rising from his chest to his neck and face. He could feel his heart racing and a throbbing in his temples. He looked at his phone and hesitated. He finally punched in a second number from memory.

"Sanchez," the voice on the other end answered.

"Alexei," Rutikov said, "I need you."

CHAPTER SEVENTEEN

Lindsey sat on the bed while she searched through video stills stored on her laptop. Aside from the videos of the exam room taken from the ceiling camera she, Jerry, and Joel had taken turns making videos of the exterior, reception area, and waiting room of the clinic. They used body-worn cameras bought from the same store, *Eye Spy U*, as the smoke detector cameras. The video from the cameras wasn't great and they had a fisheye quality to them but she thought she should be able to make out the recorded faces. There were hours and hours of video to go through. Even though she was focusing on only the clinic's employees she thought it would probably take her all day to sift through them all. And she didn't have time for that.

She needed to find Jerry and she needed to talk to Professor Canby. Joel didn't listen to her. He thought she was crazy to think the clinic was on to them. He called her paranoid. She emphatically reminded him that she had nearly been abducted and asked him for an alternate explanation which he couldn't provide. She told him they needed to be careful and maybe they should stay near one another, but he refused.

`   Lindsey interrupted her search of the videos to check her email again, like she had every few minutes for the last two hours. There was still nothing from Jerry or Canby. She checked the time on her laptop, 9:00 a.m., and briefly debated returning to the videos but dismissed the idea. Jerry was more important. In fact, he was the only thing that mattered. She closed her laptop and left it on the bed, grabbed her keys, and headed to her car. Twenty minutes later she hitting the call button on an intercom attached to an iron gate.

I drove through the open gate at Josie's house and up the cobbled drive. My father was standing at the bottom of the steps. "How the hell did he know I was on my way," I thought.

As I got out of the car I asked him just that.

"I didn't," he said, "I think the girlfriend was just here."

"What? Jerry's girlfriend? Where is she?" I said.

"She left. She asked to see Jerry so I told her what happened. She got all broken up, crying and stuff, and just left. I asked her to stay but she just took off down the driveway."

"How long ago?" I said, looking back down the drive trying to remember if I saw anyone near the gate as I pulled in.

"Just a little bit before you got here. We talked here at the bottom of the steps and I was on my way back in when you drove up."

"Did she have a car? Did you see a car?"

"No, she walked up from the gate after I buzzed it open."

"Damn it, Dad. You should have kept her here. You know I need to talk to her."

"What was I gonna do, Sam? Tie her up? She just ran off down the driveway."

"Yeah, yeah."

"Sam, I called after her. I asked her to stay."

"Yeah, okay. I guess you did what you could."

I looked down the driveway again, thinking about what to do next.

"Did she say anything? Did she say when she last saw Jerry?"

"No, she didn't say anything. Like I said, she asked for Jerry and when I told her she started crying and took off."

"That's it?"

"Yep, that's it."

"Do you think she was genuine? Really surprised?"

"Without a doubt. And on top of that she looked scared."

"Are you sure? Maybe it was just the shock of hearing about Jerry. Especially if they were close."

"Could be. My impression was she was scared though."

"That could be interesting. Did you get her name?"

"Yeah. She said her name was Lindsey. Didn't give her last name."

"Okay, good. Let's go get Jerry's phone and we'll see if she's in the contact list. Oh, and ask Josie if it's okay for us to check out the phone."

"Yeah. She's up in her room. She doesn't come down much. And I don't think she's sleeping very much either."

Inside, we walked through the living and dining rooms and into the kitchen. Dad put on a fresh pot of coffee. I grabbed a stool at the massive island. I had already decided not to let him in on what I had learned so far. There was no use getting anyone's hopes up at this stage.

I scanned the room, which was larger than Dad's entire house, and again wondered how Josie made her money.

He must have guessed what I was thinking. "Ex-husbands," he said.

"How many?"

"Two I know of. Probably more."

"What the hell did they do for a living?"

"The first dealt in some kind of high-end real estate. The second, I don't know for sure. He owned some business I think."

"She did well in the divorces."

"There were no divorces. Both died."

I gave him a sideways look while he poured the coffee into our cups.

"Don't give me that," he said. "There's no way."

I gave him a big smile and took a gulp of the coffee. He shook his head and walked off to get Jerry's phone. I called after him.

"Get the keys to the Infiniti, too."

121

A few minutes later I had her number. There were thirty or so missed calls and voicemails from her in the last day. I hit a button and the phone dialed her number. It immediately went to voicemail. I left a message telling her who I was and that I wanted to talk to her. I added I would hang onto Jerry's phone and she could get me that way.

"What are you going to do now?" Dad asked.

"I'll give Josie's car a better search. Then I'd like to borrow your car again. I've got a few things to check on."

"Sure. You going by the morgue?"

"As a matter of fact I am. Why?"

"They called here. I think it was probably your new girlfriend. How'd that go anyway?"

"Marley? She called here?"

"This woman said her name was something or other Jones. The ME's assistant. She said Jerry's body was being released and we could contact a funeral home. They'd take care of the details for us. If you swing by there you can tell them Toale Brothers Funeral Home will be there this afternoon."

"Yeah, I'll do that. And her name is Gabrielle Jones but she goes by Marley. It's her middle name. Did she say anything else?"

"No. It was all short and professional."

We both sipped our coffee.

"What kind of name is Gabrielle Jones?"

"Where are you going with that, Dad?"

"Hey, I'm just asking, you know."

"She's half Jamaican and half Seminole. And I don't want to hear another word. You got it?"

"Yeah, yeah. Okay. I was just asking."

"Enough already."

I finished my coffee and headed to the garage. I really doubted I'd find anything helpful in the car but you never knew. I took my time, checking every possible compartment and crevice. I checked under the floor mats, between and underneath the seats, and the visors. I raised the headrests and checked the vents. I found nothing. One thing I did notice that I hadn't when I drove it yesterday was the steering wheel. It was one of those telescoping types. It also had a lever to tilt up and down. The wheel was positioned as far forward and as far up as possible. The position made plenty of room for a large belly.

I finished and closed up the garage. Back inside, Dad was watching TV in the Great Room adjacent to the kitchen. Josie was still not around. I gave him the keys and told him I'd catch up with him later.

"One more thing, Dad."

"What?" he asked. He didn't take his eyes off the television.

"Can I get twenty bucks for gas?"

CHAPTER EIGHTEEN

Lindsey's car was parked with the engine running on the side of the road not far from Jerry's home. She sat in the driver's seat crying. She had worried about Jerry but never believed he might be dead. She also didn't believe it was an overdose. She knew he was murdered. Hundreds of thoughts and emotions enveloped her. She forced herself to focus. She straightened in her seat and wiped her eyes.

Jerry was caught and forced to tell them everything. The fake cop found her and had tried to abduct her because of it. They knew who she was and most likely knew of Joel and Canby too. She had to tell them about Jerry and warn them.

She pulled her phone from her purse and dialed Professor Canby's cellphone. It went to voicemail. She left a message for him to call and told him Jerry was dead. She punched the 'End' button and then texted and emailed

125

him. Both messages began with "9-1-1" to stress its importance.

She next dialed Joel's number and listened to his phone ring. As it did she thought she heard another phone ringing. She picked her head up and looked around. The man standing outside her car startled her. She hadn't noticed him walk up. The fake cop from the University pulled on the door handle. The door was half open when Lindsey dropped her phone, shifted into 'Drive' and stomped on the gas.

As the car accelerated down the road she checked the mirror. The fake cop stood in the road, watching her speed away. She debated turning off the road, zigzagging through the streets in case he tried to follow her. Instead, she decided to continue on putting as much distance between them as possible. She didn't slow the car until she arrived at the Village.

The Village was the main business district of Siesta Key and catered to vacationers. It was a short walk from the public beach and was several blocks long.   Lined with restaurants, bars, swim and souvenir shops it was always busy with tourists. Lindsey pulled down a side street and behind a convenience store. She sat in the car shaking. She tried to calm down telling herself nothing would happen here among the crowds.

She sat and thought about what she learned since she arrived at Jerry's house. They caught Jerry and killed him. Before he died he told them everything he knew. She knew he wouldn't do it unless he was forced. And now they know about her, Joel, Canby and the University. So they must know what we were doing. They must know about the videos. And of course they must know where she lived. Unless they were watching Jerry's house she was followed from her apartment. She couldn't chance going back there.

Lindsey found her phone on the floor beneath her seat. She needed to call Joel and maybe try Canby again. Her phone showed a missed call and voicemail from Jerry. Her heart skipped but she quickly concluded it was Jerry's family using his phone. She would listen to the voicemail after she called Joel.

As she dialed, she remembered hearing a phone ringing as the fake cop stood next to the car. She hung up the phone. The fake cop had Joel's phone. He had Joel.

Lindsey switched her phone off and dropped it on the other seat next to her purse. She backed out of the parking spot and began the drive to the University. She had to find Canby.

She drove past the public beach to the South Bridge leading off the key. She took the Trail north towards the

University and checked her mirrors frequently. She wasn't being followed as far as she could tell. She arrived twenty minutes later and parked in the student's lot.

She ran to the Administration building and took the elevator to the fourth floor. Minutes later she was knocking on Professor Canby's office door. Getting no response she knocked again and tried the doorknob. It was locked.

She hurried down the hall to the Journalism Admin office and in through the open door. There were numerous desks arranged facing the door. It looked much like a newspaper's city room might. None were staffed but three people, two women and a man, stood in the back of the room. They were huddled together talking.

One of the women noticed Lindsey and began walking towards her.

"Can I help you?" she said.

"I'm looking for Professor Canby. I tried his office but the door is locked. I was hoping you might tell me where I can find him," Lindsey said.

The woman paused and looked back toward her companions. The other woman nodded.

"I'm sorry, dear. We just found out this morning when we came in. Professor Canby was killed yesterday, a hit and run here on campus."

Lindsey went numb. She began to tremble. This can't be a coincidence, she thought. They're killing us all.

"Are you alright? You're shaking, dear. Come, sit down," the woman said.

She led Lindsey over to a chair near the closest desk.

"I take it you were a student of his."

"Yes," Lindsey said. "I'm in his Ethics class. What happened? Do you know what happened?"

"It's terrible. We're all in shock. He apparently was leaving campus after his class and walking to his car. He was found in the parking lot. The police said he was struck and killed by a car. They have no idea who did it. They said no one saw anything. I can't believe someone would do that and just leave. What is this world coming to?"

Lindsey stood. "What do I do?"

"Don't worry, dear. Everyone enrolled in his class will be officially withdrawn."

Lindsey looked at the woman, turned, and ran out the door.

CHAPTER NINETEEN

Leon stood on the side of the road and watched the girl speed away. That would have been too easy, he thought. He walked back to his car and got in. He debated using the kid's phone to call the girl. Maybe he could convince her he only wanted to talk to her. He dismissed that idea. She obviously talked to Jerry Manfred's family and knows he's dead. She was coming from his house. Even if she did agree to meet, she would want a public place. She might even have the cops waiting.

He decided to head back home. As he pulled a U-turn to head off the North Bridge a thumping arose from the trunk of the car.

"Knock it off, kid. Or I'll come back there and shut you up," he yelled.

Leon had to fix things. The Doc thinks he screwed up, he thought. So to make it right his plan was to grab the other kids and interrogate them. He would get any files of theirs and find out what Canby had. He'd break into his office and home if he had to.

It took Leon twenty-five minutes to get home. He backed his car into the single space garage attached to his mother's house and closed the overhead door. His mother had died several years earlier, leaving the house and its worn contents to him.

He rolled over an old wheel chair to the back of the car. He yanked the kid Joel out and flopped him onto the chair. Leon had bound Joel, hands and feet, with duct tape. He had wrapped a generous amount around his head to cover his mouth as well. The kid's clothes were soaked with sweat. He looked as pale as a Canadian tourist in January.

Leon wheeled the kid through the service door and into his kitchen. The house was dark. Leon had purposely not opened any shades this morning. He grabbed a beer from the refrigerator and filled a glass with tap water for the kid. He walked into the living room to set each down on a side table before bringing the kid in for questioning.

"Good morning," Sanchez said. He was sitting cross-legged in a wooded chair in a corner near the front window.

"What the hell, " Leon said, "Who the fuck are you?"

"Dr. Rutikov sent me to help you."

"I don't need no help. How'd you get in here?"

"You left the front door unlocked. Very unsafe."

"Bullshit. I always lock my doors."

Sanchez smiled at Leon. He stood, walked over to Leon and took the drinks from him. He set them down on the table.

"Leon, that is your name, no? My name is Alexei. Dr. Rutikov said you might protest. And I understand. You want to finish what you've started. I've been in the same position myself. Dr. Rutikov was insistent, however. He is the boss. So, let us put that behind us and get to work. I see we have an interview to do."

Leon stood, thinking. He sure didn't like this. Rutikov obviously doesn't trust him to finish the job. He made one little fuck up, big deal.

"Okay, I get it," he said. "For the record, though, I could do this myself. I don't need you."

"I'm sure. But orders are orders."

Sanchez poked his head in the kitchen then turned to face Leon.

"Let us begin. Sit. Drink your beer. I'll have the water and you can catch me up. Tell me all about these people and how they planned to disrupt Dr. Rutikov's affairs."

Leon plopped down on a ratty sofa and filled Alexei in. He made sure Alexei understood it was he, Leon, who figured out the scheme. He told him about Jerry. He told him about the videos he erased and the disks he destroyed. He told him about dumping Jerry's body and bragged about staging the scene as an overdose. He also glossed over his screw-up with Canby excusing it as taking advantage of an opportunity. He finished by explaining how he snatched Joel in the school parking lot.

"So, that is everything?" Alexei said.

"Yep. Everything."

"The girl's address?"

"On the desk over there, with the others. Next to the kid Jerry's laptop." Leon nodded towards it.

Alexei walked to the desk and examined a piece of paper. "This is all I need then," he said.

Sanchez turned and fired two shots from a silenced Beretta 9mm pistol into Leon's chest. Leon slumped in his seat and died in a puddle of spilt beer and his own urine.

Sanchez walked into the kitchen. He pushed the wheelchair with Joel into the living room. He positioned Joel in front of and facing Leon. He then sat on the sofa next to the body.

"Leon here told me your name is Joel. That is correct, yes?"

Joel, wide-eyed, stared at Leon.

"Yes, my friend?" Sanchez said.

Joel nodded slowly.

"Well, Joel. You and I have many things to talk about."

CHAPTER TWENTY

When I walked into the morgue, Marley was standing behind the counter. Dr. Cortez was standing next to her and they were both reading from a stack of papers in Marley's hand. Marley looked up and gave me a small smile. She winked and gave a nearly imperceptible nod in Cortez's direction.

"I'll be with you in a minute, sir," she said.

"Take your time," I answered.

After a few moments Cortez said something to Marley I couldn't hear. He flipped the counter, walked past me, and exited through the swinging doors. He never looked at me. I walked up to the counter. Marley was smiling widely now.

"I was hoping you'd show up today," she said.

"I forgot to get your phone number."

"Yeah, I know. I was beginning to doubt your abilities as a detective."

"It had nothing to do with that and everything to do with you distracting me."

"That's nice to know," she said. "Want a cup of coffee?"

"You bet. Cream and sugar."

"Come on. Follow me."

She came through the counter, led me through the swinging doors and down the hall. We ended up in a small room with several institutional-style tables and chairs. There was a bank of vending machines on one wall.

"My treat," she said taking several coins from her lab coat pocket.

We sat with our coffees at one of the tables.

"My dad said you called. He told me to tell you Jerry's body would be picked up this afternoon. Toale Brothers I think he said."

"Sure. That's fine." She looked down at her coffee.

"What is it?" I said.

"Nothing, I guess. Just a feeling I got when I was talking to him."

"Yeah, well, I tried to warn you about him."

"Did he say anything?" A little bit of Jamaican accent slipped as she pronounced it 'any-ting'.

"He tried to but I shut him down. Don't let it bother you."

"Okay, I'll try."

We took our coffees and headed back to the morgue.

"Oh," she said as we walked through the doors, "let me get you Jerry's personal property. I know it's not much, clothing and stuff. But you should take it with you. Come into the back with me." We went through the gap in the counter and into the business end of the morgue.

Walking into the autopsy room of a morgue always made me feel anxious. I wasn't unfamiliar with dead bodies. I had seen many with most being damaged beyond the average person's comprehension. I was numbed to the carnage years ago. However, whatever I witnessed as a police officer and detective I always knew it was a person laying at my feet. It was a human being with a family and friends who had woken up that morning oblivious to their imminent end. They laughed, cried, ate, drank, slept, and loved the same as I did. No matter who they were I always remembered that and treated the remains with respect.

I think it was the sterile environment of the morgue that unsettled me. In the morgue the bodies were treated like meat. No, that's unfair. They were treated as just another piece of evidence. Their dissection was a

137

scientific study, nothing more. It was too devoid of emotion, too clinical, for me.

A body was laying on a stainless steel table to the left. The Y-incision in its chest was stitched closed with heavy black sutures.

"That's the accident victim I mentioned last night," Marley said, walking past and towards a large bank of drawers.

"He looks pretty banged up," I said.

Marley called out from across the room. "Yes, he is. Dr. Cortez said he's sure the car backed over him a couple of times. Doc says he needs to talk to the investigators. He'll probably call it a murder."

"I'll bet. You don't accidently back over anyone three or four times."

Marley came back carrying a large plastic bag with Jerry's name on the label. Black clothing was visible through the plastic. She handed me the bag and looked down at the body.

"I agree. It happened in the parking lot of a school campus. He was a teacher, a professor. Though I don't know the difference between the two."

"I don't either. What school?"

"Middle South Florida University. It's up near the airport, on the Trail."

I tried to remember.

"I think that's where Jerry went to school," I said.

"That would be some coincidence."

I stood next to the table thinking. What would be the chances? What would be the connection, if any? I should find out what Jerry was studying and what this professor taught.

"Sam," Marley said.

"Sorry, I was thinking." I said.

"Obviously. What about?"

"I think Jerry was murdered."

"What?"

"Last night, after we left the restaurant. I drove over to the marina to take a look at the scene. I found a witness."

I told Marley about Captain Bob and what he told me.

"Have you told Detective King yet?" she said.

"No. I wanted to poke around some more, talk to Jerry's friends. Maybe see if anyone knew what he may have been doing that night. And don't forget, this Captain Bob character is homeless. He's not the most reliable witness. Plus he's pretty reluctant about talking to the police. I can't blame him seeing as a cop is involved."

"I really think you can talk to King. You can trust him."

"I don't know. I think I'm going to hang onto this for a bit." I could tell Marley didn't like that answer.

"What's this guys name?" I said.

Marley looked at the toe tag.

"Douglas Canby. Douglas Sebastian Canby," she said.

"Can you write that down for me? And your phone number too?"

I smiled at her and she smiled back.

Marley pulled out her cellphone from a pocket of her lab coat.

"What's your cell number. I'll call you then you'll have my number. And I can text you Canby's name too."

"I don't have a cellphone of my own," I said. "I'm using Jerry's right now." Marley laughed and gave me a look like I was crazy.

"You should join the human race and get one," she said.

We walked back out to the counter and she grabbed a pad of paper and began writing.

"I'm going to put my address down too. My apartment is not far from the hospital. It's right on Hillview Street just the other side of the Trail. How about

I make dinner for you tonight? I'm pretty good in the kitchen. Come around six-thirty?"

She tore the paper from the pad and handed it to me. Even under the florescent lights her green eyes sparkled.

"I'll be there."

She kissed me for the second time ever and walked in back to hang out with Douglas Canby.

CHAPTER TWENTY-ONE

After leaving the hospital I headed north on Tamiami Trail. I was hoping I could get some information on Douglas Sebastian Canby at the University. I had originally planned to look for Captain Bob after I stopped at the morgue today. Once I learned about Douglas Canby my plan changed.

As I passed the marina where Jerry had been found, I began to convince myself Canby's death was related to Jerry's. Marley said Canby teaching at the same school Jerry attended was a hell of a coincidence. I believe in coincidences. They happen all the time. But I knew one thing when it came to homicide investigations, coincidences mean you're on the right track.

On the other side of Main Street, past the marina and downtown, the neighborhood began to change much like all neighborhoods do. Low rent motels, liquor stores, and pawnshops dominated the scenery. Snuggled in along the way were the Ringling School of Art and the Ringling Museum campus. Like flowers in a field of weeds.

As I came to the airport I began watching for the entrance to the University. It came up quickly on the left and I pulled in. I parked in a lot designated for visitors. Walking towards the nearest group of buildings I saw a map in a display case. It was like one of those you might find in a shopping mall. It was a bird's-eye view of the campus with a large red dot marked 'You are here.'

I located the Administration building on the map. I knew that was where most schools housed their offices. I headed off and made it there in a few minutes. Inside I found a directory listing the various schools such as Liberal Arts and Music.

Subheadings listed various professors and instructors. Canby's was the first name listed under the School of Journalism.

I took the elevator and wandered the fourth floor until I found the Journalism Administration office. There was a small crowd of students gathered in the front of the room. A middle-aged man was talking and they were all listening attentively. I walked over to the closest desk. The woman seated behind it looked up at me.

"Can I help you?"

"Yes," I said. "I'd like to get some information on Douglas Canby. I'm in the right place, right?"

"Oh, we thought someone from the police might be by again."

She stood and walked to the back of the room. She leaned over and spoke with another woman seated at another desk. At one point she gestured toward me. When she came back she told me the University was happy to cooperate any way they could. She asked what I needed. At no point did she ask to see any identification. For an employee of an institution of higher learning she wasn't too sharp, I thought. I wasn't going to let this opportunity slip away.

"Did Professor Canby have a private office? I'd like to take a look at it." I said.

"Yes. Isn't that unusual though? It happened outside. I thought it was an accident."

"Yes, we're operating on that premise. I'm just covering all the bases. We have to dot all the 'i's and cross the 't's."

"Of course. Let me show you. Follow me, please."

She led me down the hall to his office, unlocked the door, and flipped on the light switch. She stepped aside to let me enter. It was a small office made smaller by the over-sized oak desk taking up most of the floor space.

144

There were books and papers piled on the desk as well as a desktop computer and monitor. Wall mounted shelves on every wall were also crammed with books, binders, and papers.

"Do you mind if I look around a bit?" I said.

"No. Go right ahead. Is there anything specific your looking for? Maybe I can help."

"No, not really," I said. "But what would help is a list of the classes he taught."

"He was only teaching one class this semester. An ethics class."

"Is there a list of students enrolled in his class? A roster I might be able to look at?"

"Yes, of course. It's in the other office. Let me get you a copy." She turned and left me alone.

While she was gone I poked around. I shuffled through things on the desk and looked through the drawers. I had no idea what I was looking for. I hoped if there were anything it would jump out at me.

He had a terrible filing system. One drawer was crammed with unlabeled folders another with unlabeled CDs or DVDs. I couldn't tell one from the other. The middle drawer was full of pens, pencils, paper clips and markers. Nothing struck me as relevant.

The computer was on and a screen saver that looked like a star field was running. I moved the mouse and a box popped up asking for a password. I wasn't going to guess. The best thing to do was leave it alone. If it came to it, police crime labs usually had a computer forensics section that could get through that.

The woman returned carrying a single piece of paper. "Here you go. I made this copy for you. You can keep it."

"Thanks," I said, taking it from her. I scanned the list. It was in alphabetical order by last name. I went right to the 'M's. Gerald Manfred was the first of them. This was more than a coincidence. I needed to find out if the connection ran deeper.

"I don't think I need any more today," I said. "Would it be alright to come back if I think of something else?"

"Yes, of course."

"Thank you. And, I'm sorry, I should have asked your name earlier."

"Pamella. Just ask for me."

As I walked back to the Cadillac, I went through the entire list of names. Near the bottom was the only Lindsey, Lindsey Wellington. I was sure that was no coincidence.

When I got back to the car I pulled out Jerry's phone and called Lindsey. It went to voicemail again. I left another message, this one more urgent than the last. Considering her relationship to Jerry, she might be involved in whatever all this was about.

I checked the clock on the dashboard. It was close to four. I headed back the way I came. It would take me by the marina so I figured I could still take a quick look for Captain Bob. I should still have time to get home and shower and change clothes before heading to Marley's for dinner.

CHAPTER TWENTY-TWO

Lindsey couldn't stop running. She ran out the door of the Administration building and through the campus. She ran until she couldn't run anymore. She was in the Quad. Students walked around her. Some were walking alone, some in groups heading in every direction. She plopped down on the ground, panting. She had to calm down and think about what she needed to do. She needed somewhere safe, near people. She looked around and saw the Student Union. She inhaled deeply and ran the entire distance. She stopped only when she got to the cafeteria. She took a table by herself near a group of students.

It all was unbelievable to her. They were killing them all to keep them quiet. They knew that Canby, Jerry, Joel, and she were going to expose them. They would all go to jail.

But it wasn't just that they knew. It was the evidence. They knew about the video and audio evidence.

They needed it all to guarantee they were safe. They would have Jerry's laptop and the cameras and probably his disks. They needed the other copies though. They each had a complete set, five DVDs. Canby kept his in his office. Joel's she couldn't be sure about. He probably had them at his place, like hers were at her apartment.

They may even have Canby's already. She needed to find out and would somehow have to retrieve them. They may also have Joel's copies by now. They may even have hers, and her laptop.

But maybe not, she thought. Maybe they don't have hers yet. If she could get her copies, and Jerry's too, she could go to the police and show them. They could protect her. She would tell them about Professor Canby's plan to expose the clinic. She could show them the video as proof. She would also have to tell them they broke the law by breaking into the clinic. She would get in trouble and maybe even go to jail, but it was better than getting killed.

Lindsey could hear the students at the next table talking. They were talking about Professor Canby. None of them seemed to have been in any of his classes. One of the girls was saying how horrible it was. That it wasn't even safe to walk through the parking lots anymore.

One of the boys said he heard Canby was a real dick of a teacher. He said he was willing to bet one of his students ran him over. He laughed and the girl told him he was ignorant.

Lindsey decided she would have to go back to her apartment after all. It would be dangerous to do. It would be the best place for the fake cop to find her again. But she needed to get her computer and disks.

She would find a good spot to park. Far enough away to watch for a while and be sure it was safe to go in. She could take her time. She had nowhere else to go. But first she would try to get into Canby's office. She should check for his copies first.

She left the Student Union and walked back to the Administration building. She tried to think of how she would get into the locked office. She had no idea how, nor the tools, to pick a lock. She didn't think anyone there would just let her in. And they certainly would not let her leave with disks that belonged to the Professor. She would need to somehow scam her way in.

The elevator door opened on the fourth floor, a man waiting to get on stepped aside to let her off. Walking through the hall she saw the woman from the Admin office closing Canby's office door. She had keys in her hand.

Lindsey ran up to her while trying her best to look frantic. She wouldn't need to try very hard. She hoped she could distract the woman so that she would forget to lock the door.

"Please," she said and grabbed the woman by the hand. "Please help me."

"What is it, dear? What's wrong?" The woman Pamella turned from the door.

"Please. I'm in trouble." Lindsey began tugging Pamella's hand, pulling her towards the Admin office. Pamella followed along, letting Lindsey lead her away.

"I need your help. We need to get to your office."

"Okay, dear. I'm coming. What's going on?"

Lindsey saw it was working and kept the woman's hand in hers, quickening her pace. She didn't speak again until they were in the Administration Office.

Lindsey turned to the woman. "My Grade Point Average," she said. "You have to withdraw me from Professor Canby's class. An Incomplete with ruin my GPA."

"Don't worry, dear. I told your earlier, everyone in his class will get withdrawn. Weren't you listening?"

"When? When will it be done?"

"I don't know. Soon I'm sure. Please don't worry."

"Can we ask someone? Can you find out when? Please?"

"Okay, I'll ask. But don't worry. Your GPA will be fine. Just wait here for a minute."

The woman walked away from Lindsey and to the back of the office. Lindsey waited until the woman was looking away and hurried out the door. She ran down the hall to Canby's office and turned the handle. It was unlocked. She entered and locked the door behind her.

Even though the windowless office was dark she didn't switch on the lights. The light from the computer screensaver was enough to see by. She quickly scanned the desktop. Finding nothing she moved to the drawers. She found the disks in the second one she opened. She put the five unlabeled DVDs in her purse and closed the drawers.

Canby might have copied them to his computer, she thought. There was nothing she could do about that, though. She wasn't going to spend the time looking for the files and deleting them. She moved away from the desk without touching the computer.

She opened the door a crack and peered out. She slipped into the hall, gently closed the door behind her, and made it to the elevator unseen. Minutes later she was walking through the campus heading to her car.

Lindsey drove to her apartment. It was on the first floor of a two-story long, narrow building several miles from campus. She parked down the block and just around the corner. She settled in, adjusting her seat back. The sky to the west was orange. It would be dark soon. Lindsey watched her door. She yawned and rested her head against the window as she thought about Jerry.

CHAPTER TWENTY-THREE

I struck out at the marina. I didn't find Bob. The few homeless guys I did find didn't know him or were lying to protect him. I got home, showered and changed, and headed back out. The route to Marley's house would take me past Josie's place so I decided to stop. I had plenty of time to catch Dad up, get home and change, and then head over to Marley's place.

When I got there Dad walked me out back to the patio. Josie was there lying in a lounge chair. She was wrapped in a robe and staring out to the waters of the Intracoastal Waterway beyond her pool. We walked over and sat down next to her. Her eyes were red and puffy.

"Hello, Sam," she said.

"Josie, Sam tells me he has some news," Dad said.

Josie looked at me. She was hollowed out by her grief.

"Josie, I don't think Jerry was using drugs. I don't think his death was accidental. I think he was murdered."

"My God. Oh, my God." she said. Tears welled up in her eyes.

"I found someone, a witness. He told me he saw someone else drive your car into the marina's parking lot. He broke the window and left. Jerry was already in the car, in the back seat."

"Who is he? Why did he do it?"

"I don't know that yet. I think it might have something to do with Jerry's school or people from his school. Another person, a teacher, was killed yesterday in a hit and run. Jerry was in his class. I think their deaths are related."

"His school? I don't understand. How could that be?"

"I don't know that yet either. I need to talk to his girlfriend. I think she was in the same class, a journalism class. Dad talked to her earlier but she didn't say anything. I called her a few times. Her number is in Jerry's phone. I haven't gotten through yet. I'm going to keep trying. If I don't get through soon, I'll stop at her house. Her address is in Jerry's contact list on his phone."

"Should we call the police, Sam?" Dad said.

"No, not yet. I need more before we can go to them. The witness is reluctant to talk to them. I need to convince him otherwise." I didn't want to tell Josie the police might be involved.

"Thank you, Sam. Thank you for helping," Josie said. "And Sam?"

"Yes, Josie?"

Her face hardened. "Get him. Get the man that hurt my Jerry."

"I will," I said.

Dad and I left Josie alone and walked to the front door.

"Listen," I said, "I didn't want to say anything in front of Josie. The guy who dumped Jerry's body and the car might be a cop. The witness says he wore a uniform."

"What the hell?"

"That's why I don't want to call the police yet. I don't know which agency he works for or who else might be involved."

"What now? What's next?" Dad said.

"Maybe Lindsey has some answers. If she calls or comes by again let me know right away."

"Yeah, sure, of course.

"Where are you going now?" Dad said.

I wasn't going to tell him about my date with Marley. I just said I was going to get something to eat then head home to sleep.

"You're staying with Josie?" I said.

"Yeah. Oh, and tomorrow I made an appointment to get the window in Josie's car fixed. I'll need to get picked up after I drop it off. Can you do that?"

"Sure, just call me on Jerry's phone. What time do you think?"

"Later in the day. And the day after that is Jerry's funeral. Just a simple service Josie says."

"Okay, let me know the time and address later."

"Yeah."

I started down the stairs. Dad called after me.

"Jerry, do you really think this is all about school or something?"

"I don't know but I'm going to find out."

CHAPTER TWENTY-FOUR

Joel was exhausted. His shoulders and legs ached. His hands and feet were swollen from being bound. He wanted to move and adjust his position in the chair but he was too tired.

"Joel, my friend, you have done well. The added benefit for you is that you spared yourself much pain," Sanchez said. "But we still have work to do. Do you understand?"

Joel sat with his chin on his chest and eyes closed.

"Joel, are you sleeping? Wake up. We have more to do."

Joel picked his head up. "But I told you everything. I don't know anything else."

"Yes, I believe you. You have enlightened me and that knowledge is a great thing. But knowledge without action is futile. Do you know who said that?"

"What? No. I don't understand."

Sanchez chuckled. "I don't know either. I saw it on a poster hanging in a library once. It doesn't matter. What matters is that you must help me act on that knowledge."

"I don't understand."

"You see, Joel, not only do you and your friends know what Dr. Rutikov is doing, you have evidence of it. Now I believe Dr. Rutikov is performing a great service. He is responsible for alleviating great suffering in people who need it most. Many of these people cannot afford to pay for this help. Insurance does not do enough. So in order to continue helping these people he must bend the rules at times. He must sell to people who will pay much more than the drugs are worth. People who use the drugs for the wrong reason. But this is a good thing, an honorable thing. He must be allowed to continue. Don't you agree?"

Joel looked at Sanchez through tired eyes.

"Tell me you agree, Joel."

"I agree."

"Good. So, to that end I must collect all the videos you and your friends have. I will need your help to do that. Will you help me, Joel?"

From his spot on the sofa Sanchez raised the gun in his lap and pointed it at Joel's chest.

"I'll do what you want," Joel said. "I don't want to die." Tears began to form in his eyes.

"And I do not want to kill you, Joel. We are friends now, yes? We have spent many hours here today getting to know one another.

"Leon here, on the other hand, did not care to make friends. He became the sharp end of the stick when he did not need to be. As the saying goes, he would rather shoot first and ask questions later. That became detrimental to the end Dr. Rutikov wishes for.

"And this," Sanchez said as he gestured towards Leon's body next to him, "is what happens when Dr. Rutikov becomes displeased."

Joel began sobbing and tears flowed down his cheeks.

"Joel, my new friend, cheer up. Let us make a bargain. You agree to help me recover all the videos and, when I have them, I will not kill you."

"Yes, please yes," Joel said. "But what about Lindsey?"

Sanchez moved forward on the sofa and rested his elbows on his knees. "Ah, Lindsey. If Lindsey behaves I will make the same bargain with her. It will be her choice. But that comes later. First, let us talk about your disks and computer. You have copies on your computer, yes?"

"No, I didn't copy them. I just have a set of disks. But I was making a timeline. There are reports on my computer. Dates and times when things we thought were important happened."

"Good, Joel. You continue to do well for yourself. You did not try to hide that from me. I am pleased."

Sanchez stood, stretched, and yawned. He switched on the lamp sitting on top of a side table.

"But I need a break. I think you do too, Joel. You look uncomfortable. Unfortunately you must stay like this for a little while longer because I am hungry. Are you hungry? I would think you are. I would like Thai I think. Yes, Thai food. I will get Thai food and you will wait here, Joel."

Sanchez wheeled Joel into a bedroom, taped his mouth again, and closed the door behind him. Before he left, he went to the desk in the living room and put Lindsey's address in his pocket.

CHAPTER TWENTY-FIVE

On the drive to Marley's place I stopped and picked up a six-pack of light beer. I didn't want to arrive empty-handed but I didn't have enough for a decent bottle of wine. I pulled into a parking spot down the block and made the short walk to her apartment.

It was on the second floor of an 'L' shaped building with steps leading up on both ends. Hers was the end unit on the short side of the 'L'. I knocked and waited. Marley opened the door with a big smile on her face.

"You're late," she said, giving me a quick peck on the lips.

"Only a few minutes. Here, I brought this." I held out the six-pack.

"Thank you. I'll put it in the fridge, and you can help yourself when you're ready."

She took it from me and led me into her living room. Seated on the sofa was an older woman wearing a wildly floral Mumu style dress. On an easy chair across from her was Detective Nosmo King.

"I hope you don't mind but I invited my aunt and uncle to join us. My Auntie wanted to meet you."

I turned towards Marley. She had a soft smile on her face. She avoided eye contact with me and hurried towards the kitchen.

"Big city Detective Sam Laska," Nosmo King said. He stood and crossed his arms. He held a bottle of beer in one meaty hand.

"Nosmo," the woman said, "You be nice." She had a pronounced Jamaican accent.

Nosmo King looked at the woman. He turned back to me, "This is my wife, Victoria. You can call her Mrs. King."

Victoria stood and put out her hand, "No, darlin'. You call me Vicky. You can call my husband Nosmo or Nono, like his niece does."

"It better be Nosmo," he said.

I took her hand and said, "And please call me Sam."

I turned to Nosmo and stuck out my hand, "Good to see you again, Nosmo." He didn't look as pleased to see me.

After we shook he plopped back down in his chair. Vicky patted the seat next to her and motioned for me to sit. I settled in as she looked me over, up and down.

"My, you are a pretty one," Vicky said. She called out to Marley in the kitchen, "Marley, honey, your man, he's a pretty one." She pronounced it 'mon'.

"I know, Auntie," Marley called back from the kitchen.

Vicky laughed. Nosmo said, "Who says he's her man? Marley says they just met yesterday. That's not enough time to call them a couple"

"Time don't matter none, Nosmo," Vicky said, "where the heart is concerned. They together. Whether it's two days or two years. He's her man and she's his woman."

They went on with that for a while. I excused myself to get a beer and walked into the kitchen. Marley was stirring a pot on the stove. She wore blue jeans and a peasant blouse pulled down around bare shoulders. She was barefoot. She turned her head and looked at me.

"Don't be mad," she said.

"I'm not, but you could have given me a heads up."

"Probably, but I wasn't sure you'd come if I did." Marley put down the wooden spoon in her hand and turned away from the stove. "Uncle Nono is a good man.

You should tell him what you found out. He'll listen to what you have to say."

"What does he know so far? What did you tell him?"

"Nothing. He doesn't know anything. He just thinks this is a 'getting to know you' dinner."

"Okay, I'll talk to him later. I don't think he'll change his mind much."

"Maybe, maybe not." Marley turned back to the stove. "We're okay then?" she said.

"Of course," I said. She smiled.

I opened the fridge and pulled a beer from the six-pack I brought. "So, what's for dinner? It smells great in here."

"A Jamaican feast. Jerk chicken, rice and peas, and fried plantains. I had to bake the chicken, though. I can't grill here. It's against the condo rules. Now, you go back in there and get to know my family. Dinner will be ready in ten minutes."

In the living room I sat in my spot next to Marley's aunt. Nosmo and she were still bickering about whether two days makes a couple or not. That continued until Marley called us into the dining room for dinner.

As we took our seats Marley brought out the food. The aroma of garlic, allspice, and cinnamon along with the starchy sweetness of the plantains filled the room. Nosmo didn't wait and began to dig in. Vicky gave him a look that he ignored.

The food was good, really good. Marley was a great cook and I told her so.

"You're just hungry," Marley said.

"No, well yes, I am. But this is fantastic. I told you, Chicago has great restaurants and this is just as good as any of them."

She and Vicky smiled, Vicky showing her perfect white teeth.

As we ate Marley and Vicky explained that mealtimes in Jamaica are social events. The meal was secondary to the company around the table and the conversation. So we talked as we ate. We talked about work and family and friends. Vicky was the only sister of Marley's father. She had moved to Arcadia after Marley's mother died to help out. She met Nosmo there and they moved to Sarasota when Marley was old enough. A few years after that Marley's father died and Nosmo helped get her a job with the ME's office.

I told them about my dad but avoided talking about too many of his faults. I told a few funny cop stories and Nosmo kicked in a few of his.

When everyone had finished with dinner Marley and Vicky began clearing the table. Marley snuck a look at me and nodded her head. I figured this was my cue. Nosmo and I moved to the living room.

"Nosmo, I want to talk to you about Jerry, my friend's grandson."

"Lord, not again. Wait, did Marley set this up?"

"Yeah, I think so. But hear me out. I stopped by the marina the other night to look at the scene."

"What the hell did you do that for?"

"I made a promise to my friend. I want to do all I can. Can I just tell you about it?"

Nosmo rolled his eyes and settled back in his chair. "Yeah, sure. Go ahead."

"I found a witness."

"What? Who?"

I told him about Captain Bob. I told him about the car being driven into the marina lot, the window being broken, and the phone call to the police. I told him about Bob's vivid description of the offender. I also told him he might be a police officer.

Nosmo listened, leaning forward in his chair as I talked. When I finished he sat back. He paused a minute before speaking again.

"Why didn't you bring him in to me?"

"I wanted to. He refused. He said he was afraid because the guy was a cop. He told me that if I brought him in he would say he made up the whole thing."

"Okay, makes sense. But you know his story is suspect, right? Street people are not reliable witnesses. I mean, is he an alcoholic or doper? Is he delusional or have mental problems?"

"I don't know, and I get your point. I did go back to look for him again. I couldn't find him."

Nosmo gave me a shrug like 'what did you expect'.

"There's something else, too," I said. "When I stopped back at the hospital morgue to talk to Marley there was a hit and run victim there. The ME told Marley it looked like someone drove over him a couple times, probably intentionally. Just by accident Marley mentioned he was a college professor. He taught at MSFU up by the airport. That's where Jerry went to school. Jerry was in his class. I've got the roster."

"And you think both cases are related?"

"I'm saying it's a hell of a coincidence."

"I'll agree with you on that. But it's still just a coincidence. There's no solid evidence of a connection. There's no evidence this Bob character is telling the truth, either. You believe him though, right?"

"I've interviewed hundreds of witnesses in my time. He was good. He was detailed and lucid when I talked to him. I also see the flaws here. Everything you say about him being a drunk or a doper could be true. He would not be the best witness on the stand. But consider this, if I'm right you have multiple murders here. Connected by who knows what."

Nosmo stood up. "I'm gonna get another beer. You want one?"

"No, no thanks."

He left the room and I sat back, thinking about Captain Bob and Douglas Canby. Nosmo came back with his beer. He plopped back down in his chair.

"There's just not enough to call Jerry a homicide," he said.

I was about to protest. Nosmo held up a hand.

"But," he said, "I'm going to hold off closing out the case as an OD. I'll check with the guys handling the hit and run and see what they have. And I'll look for this Captain Bob. I'll pass the word to the uniforms too. It's likely someone has run into him before. If you find him first bring him to me. Okay?"

"Are you sure that's a good idea? I mean about the uniforms? This bad guy might be a cop, right?"

"No. No Police Departments in the area have officers that wear white uniform shirts. I'd bet on him being a security guard or something."

"I hadn't thought of that," I said. "Nosmo, are you starting to believe me?"

"Yeah, maybe," Nosmo said. He took a big gulp from his beer. "You're gonna do more than just look for Bob, aren't you?"

"Yeah. I think so."

We sat quiet, looking at each other. Nosmo spoke first.

"You still own a gun?"

"Yes."

"Maybe you should start carrying it. Marley says she likes you a lot."

We got called back to the dining room. Marley made a dessert, rice pudding with lime and cinnamon, and a strong coffee she called Blue Mountain. Nosmo had two helpings of pudding. When we finished, Vicky picked up her purse and told Nosmo they were leaving. They thanked Marley for dinner and said their goodbyes to us.

On their way out the door Nosmo said to me, "Don't stay long." Vicky punched him in the arm and told him to mind his manners, giving me a wink as she left.

Marley grabbed my hand and led me back to the living room. After lighting a few candles and dimming the lamp she said, "I'm going to open a bottle of wine." She walked to the kitchen and came back a few minutes later with two glasses of red.

We sat next to each other on the sofa. She snuggled close.

"I heard you and Uncle Nono talking. Did you work it out with him?"

"Yes. You were right. He actually kind of gave me his blessing to keep digging."

"I'm glad. You were a fool to doubt me." She smiled.

She took my glass from me and put both on the coffee table. We kissed, softly at first but quickly growing more urgent and intense. She tasted of sweet banana and vanilla. We pulled each other closer, both of us wrestling for control. She threw a leg over me and straddled me, unbuttoning my shirt as we kissed.

"I thought there was a three date rule," I said between kisses.

"This is our third date, the restaurant, my coffee break, and tonight. That makes three," she said.

"Your coffee break counts?"

"Do you want to argue?"

171

"No, I'm good."

We tugged and pulled at each other's clothing like it was a contest. We fell to the floor, bumping the table and knocking over our wine. We made frantic love in the puddle.

After, we showered together and moved to the bedroom. We made love again, slower and more tenderly, exploring each other, studying each other's bodies. We were in no rush this time. Later we fell asleep holding one another.

CHAPTER TWENTY-SIX

The sunlight peeked over the rooftops of the buildings to the east. It spilled into Lindsey's car through her front windshield. It woke her. She jerked upright in her seat, disoriented. She looked around, back and forth, and realized where she was. She rubbed her eyes, upset with herself for falling asleep. She looked towards her apartment. Nothing had changed. The doors were still closed and the shades on the window drawn. But why would anything be different, she thought. If someone had broken into her apartment, she might not know until she went in herself.

She looked up and down the street trying to decide if anything was out of place. It was early and the street was quiet. She never really paid attention to any of her neighbors or their cars. Nothing looked familiar but nothing looked unfamiliar either. At least she didn't have to do this in the dark.

She got out of her car taking her purse and keys with her but leaving the doors unlocked in case she needed to escape quickly. She kept her head on a swivel watching for anything and everything. She hurried to her door, keys in hand, to minimize the chance of the fat cop grabbing her on the street. She put the key in the lock. She hesitated, thinking he could be waiting for her inside.

Lindsey held her breath and threw the door open. It slammed against the inside wall. She stood in the doorway waiting, ready to run to her car. When nothing happened, no boogeyman jumped out, she carefully entered. She moved into the living room and left the door open, just in case.

Everything was as she left it. The furniture wasn't overturned, no drawers emptied out onto the floors. She went through the small dining area and the kitchen. Nothing was out of place. She went to her bedroom.

He had been there. The mattress, twisted to the side, was hanging off the bed. The bed linens had been tossed on the floor. The drawers of her dresser had been emptied onto the floor and stacked haphazardly in the corner of the room. Her desk was pulled away from the wall and it's drawers also emptied onto the floor. Her closet door was open and her clothes discarded on the floor inside.

The chaos in the room froze her where she stood. She slowly entered, taking it all in. Panic set in and she rushed to the bed. She had left her laptop there. She dug through the mess of bedclothes on the floor around her. She sifted through what were the contents of her desk drawers. She stood and pushed the mattress aside.

It was gone. They were gone. Her computer and her copies of the videos were gone. There was nothing more to do here. Nothing more she could do. She still had Canby's copies and Jerry's might still be at his house. Canby's office or Jerry's house would be the next target of the fat cop.

Lindsey hurried to her closet and picked out a fresh blouse and jeans. She grabbed a handful of clean underwear from the floor in front of her dresser and stuffed them into her purse. She went to the bathroom next, putting shampoo and soap into her purse as well. She didn't need makeup.

She went through the kitchen and dining area and into the living room on her way out. She stopped twenty feet from the front door, halted by fear. There, blocking her exit was a man.

CHAPTER TWENTY-SEVEN

Marley pushed closer, waking me. I was spooning her, my arm across her breasts and face nuzzled in the back of her neck. Her hair fell across my eyes.

"I have to go to work." She said.

"I don't want you to go."

"I can tell." She said snuggling closer. She rolled over and faced me. She was smiling. "You can stay here. Wait for me until I get back."

"I have things to do too, I guess."

"I know, wishful thinking." She jumped from the bed and scurried to the bathroom closing the door behind her. I heard the shower working. I thought about joining her but decided against it. The closed door meant I wasn't invited I said to myself.

I threw my pants on and waddled barefoot to the kitchen to make a pot of coffee. I poured a cup and moved to the living room to give Marley some privacy. The wine glasses were still on the wet floor. I set my coffee down and cleaned up the mess.

I drew the front curtains and opened a window. The morning was cool and the fresh air felt good. I opened a few more, front and back, to catch the cross breeze. I sipped my coffee as I watched the sun rise over the neighborhood. It was the first time I had seen it in over a year. When I heard Marley in the kitchen, I went over to join her.

She wore light blue scrubs and a white lab coat. She was sipping a cup of coffee from a to-go cup.

"Thanks for making it," she said. "You make good coffee."

"Thanks. If there's one thing cops know, it's how to make coffee." We stood across the room from each other smiling.

"Do you mind if I take a shower before I leave? Do I have the time?" I said.

"Actually, I have to get to work. But you can stay, just lock up and close the windows when you go. I'll give you my key. Just come by the hospital and drop it off later."

"Are you sure?"

"Yep. I'm sure. And that way I get to see you again." She put her coffee down and took a ring of keys from her pocket. As she unhooked a key she said, "There are fresh towels under the sink."

She handed me the key and I walked her to the door. We kissed, a long and tender kiss. As she opened the door to go I said, "Marley." She turned to me. "When we met the other day at the hospital, I thought you were out of my league."

"Silly," she said. "Of course I am."

And she was gone.

I took a shower and had another cup of coffee while I dressed. I rinsed out my cup and the coffee pot and wiped down the counter. I left, double-checking the door lock as I did.

Sitting in the car I ran down the things I thought I needed to do today. First, I needed to find Captain Bob and Lindsey, pick up Dad when he called, and drop Marley's key off at the hospital. It was a full day by my current standards. I decided to call Lindsey first. I pulled out Jerry's phone and dialed the number. It went straight to voicemail again. Frustrated, I didn't leave a message. I looked her up in the contacts again and checked her address. Her place was a few miles north and east. I started the car and headed in that direction.

Twenty minutes later I was driving down her street checking the house numbers. The neighborhood was filled with low-rise, multi-unit buildings with the occasional single-family house tucked in. I found Lindsey's building a little more than halfway down the block on the north side of the street. The front door of one apartment on the ground floor was wide open. I parked the car and walked over. It was hers.

Open doors weren't often a good sign. Few people leave their doors wide open, particularly without a screen door. It was an invitation to trouble and especially so in a transient neighborhood. I stood in the doorway and looked inside. Everything seemed fine but I was still cautious. I checked the door lock for damage. There was none. I took one step inside and stood in a small foyer that was open to the living room.

I was about to call out to see if anyone was home when a girl hurried into the room from somewhere else in the apartment. She was a mess. Her hair was a tangle of curls. Her mascara was smeared onto her cheeks and her clothes looked like they had been slept in. Clothing was hanging out of the purse she carried. She stopped in her tracks. Her eyes went wide and her mouth fell open.

"Lindsey?" I said. She didn't answer. Her eyes fixed on the door behind me.

"You *are* Lindsey, right? My name is Sam. I'm a friend of Jerry's grandmother. You talked to my father yesterday at her house."

"Thank God," she said. "You scared me."

"You shouldn't leave your door open like that."

"I thought I might have to leave in a hurry."

"Lindsey, can I come in? Can we talk?"

"Who are you again?"

"A friend of Jerry's grandmother. She asked me to find out what happened to Jerry. I was a police officer, a detective, in Chicago. I think Jerry was murdered and I think you can help me find out who did it."

Lindsey dropped to the floor, sitting cross-legged, and began crying. She looked up at me. "It's our own fault. We did this," she said between sobs.

"What happened, Lindsey? Tell me what happened."

CHAPTER TWENTY-EIGHT

Joel was again facing the dead body of Leon when he woke. He had slept, restlessly, still taped to the wheelchair. Sanchez had returned with the promised Thai food the evening before and, after he ate, he fed Joel. After four or five fork-fulls he retched. He liked Pad Thai but it wasn't the food that was tying his stomach in knots. It was fear. The smell from Leon's body wasn't helping either. It stunk of stale beer, urine, and something like raw meat left in the sun for a few days.

Sanchez had told Joel he had visited Lindsey's apartment and had found her computer and disks. Lindsey was not home however. Joel asked if Sanchez would now leave Lindsey out of it but he did not answer.

Joel smelled coffee and heard Sanchez in the kitchen. Soon after Sanchez wheeled Joel to a table in the kitchen and cut the tape holding his arms to the chair.

"Here, Joel. I made some toast and coffee for breakfast. Maybe now you can eat without vomiting. You need your strength today. We must retrieve your computer and disks."

Joel took a sip of the bitter coffee and made a face.

"What is it, Joel? You do not like the coffee?" Sanchez said.

"No, I mean, I don't like coffee. Any coffee. Can I have a glass of water instead?"

"Yes, of course Joel." Sanchez smiled and brought Joel a glass of tap water. Joel drank and nibbled on a piece of toast.

"Tell me again about your roommate, Joel. Does he know about your business? Does he know about the videos?"

"No, like I told you, we're just roommates. I didn't tell him about it. We were keeping it a secret. The Professor told us not to tell anyone."

"You are sure about this? You are telling me the truth?"

"Yes. Yes, I wouldn't lie to you."

"Good, Joel. But I must make sure. Do you know his schedule, when he will be away from home? In class, for example."

"Yeah, I think so. He's usually gone until two o'clock most every day."

"Good. That is good. This roommate, what is his name again?"

"Lou, Louis. His name is Louis."

"Are you lovers?" Sanchez smiled.

"What? No, not at all. Why would you think that?"

"I must be sure, Joel. Lovers tell each other their secrets."

"No, no way. I'm not gay. No way. We just live together. It's cheaper, you know, if we share rent and stuff."

"Yes, I understand," Sanchez said. He again sat on the sofa next to Leon's body, crossing his legs. "Do you understand the reason I ask about this roommate of yours, Joel?"

"I think so," Joel said. He took another sip of water.

"I must make sure no one is home when I go there to retrieve your computer and disks. So, is this roommate Louis home now?"

"Like I said, he's gone until two every day. He leaves to go to class about eight-thirty. I...I don't know what time it is now, but if it's after that he won't be home."

Sanchez glanced at his watch. "So then. He will not be home. I hope he is not."

Sanchez stood and looked down at Joel. "I will go then and come back with those things. You will wait here. Unfortunately I will need to bind your hands again and tape your mouth."

Sanchez did just that and took Joel's keys from the desk. He rolled Joel back into the bedroom and left Leon's house.

CHAPTER TWENTY-NINE

I walked over to Lindsey and sat on the floor across from her. She looked up at me and wiped tears from her eyes and cheeks.

"We did this," she said. "We were trying to catch them selling narcotics illegally."

"Who, Lindsey?"

"The Manasota Pain Management Clinic. We thought they were selling oxycodone and Percocet and other drugs to addicts by writing bogus prescriptions. And we were right. We've got the evidence. But Professor Canby wanted more."

"This Professor Canby, you were all in his Journalism class?"

"Yes. This was all his idea, you know. I think he wanted to do this for his ego. He missed out on a Pulitzer Prize once and he thought this was his ticket to winning it. He was going to do an exclusive for the newspaper. He wanted to make a big splash like that university in Illinois

185

did proving wrongful convictions. He recruited Joel and myself and I convinced Canby to let Jerry in. He made it a special project. He promised to recommend us for internships with a newspaper or TV station if we were successful.

"Oh Jesus, poor Jerry. It's all my fault he's dead." Lindsey began sobbing again. "We never thought this could happen. We knew it was a risk and there was a chance we could get caught, but we never thought it would come to this."

I took her hand. "It's not your fault, Lindsey. Don't think that. Don't ever think that." I took her by the shoulders and helped her into a chair.

"What was the plan, Lindsey?"

"Well, first we wore hidden cameras and microphones and scouted the clinic out. We figured out that everyone coming to the clinic had to see the doctor and then they were given a prescription. We were going to make appointments for ourselves but Professor Canby didn't want that. He said we wouldn't be able to use the cameras or mics because the doctor might actually do an exam. We were stuck. We had to get into the exam rooms but didn't know how.

"Then Jerry came up with an idea. He found a place on-line that sold hidden video cameras, cameras that

186

were disguised like everyday objects. You know, like radios, teddy bears, clocks, and stuff."

"Teddy bears?" I said.

"Yeah, lots of people use them to check up on their baby sitters. Anyway, Jerry got cameras that look like smoke detectors. He said he could sneak into the clinic after hours and plant them on the ceiling."

"And he did?"

"Yeah, Canby loved that idea. So Jerry did and that's how we got the evidence. The problem is the cameras don't have a long battery life and had to get changed every so often. Jerry handled that too."

"Was that what he was supposed to do the other night?"

Lindsey's head dropped. "Yes. He was supposed to meet us at class the next day and let us know everything was cool. When he didn't, I started to worry. I called and called but I couldn't get hold of him."

"So you came to the house to look for him and found out."

"Yes. But there's more."

Lindsey told me everything. She told me about the uniformed man who tried to take her on campus and then approached her again as she left Josie's house. She told me she suspected Joel had been abducted, and about learning of Canby's death. She told me about getting into his office to retrieve the videodisks and, finally, about her bedroom being ransacked and her computer and disks being taken.

"This guy in the uniform, can you describe him to me?" I said.

Lindsey thought for a moment. Then said, "He was a white guy. Older, in his forties I think. He was fat too, with a big belly. He wasn't very tall though, maybe five-eight or five-nine. His hair was brown I think, and kind of shaggy. You know, uncombed. Oh, and he stunk too. He had terrible body odor."

Lindsey made a face like she smelled him all over again.

"What did the uniform look like?"

"The shirt was white and he had a gold badge of some kind pinned to it. I didn't get a good look at it. And his pants were dark, maybe dark blue or black. And his shoes were black I think."

"Did you see any patches on the sleeves?"

"I think there were, but I wasn't really paying attention. I was pretty scared."

"I think you had a right to be." I told Lindsey about Captain Bob and what he saw. "It sure sounds like the guy who accosted you is the same one that…left Jerry at the Marina."

Tears began streaming down Lindsey's cheeks and she was trembling again. She wrapped her arms around herself.

"Lindsey," I said, "You're safe now." I put a hand on her shoulder.

"But Jerry..." she said.

"There's nothing you could have done to prevent his death. But there is something you can do now. You can help me catch this fucker."

Lindsey looked up at me. She put on a brave face, wiped her eyes, and said, "Yeah, let's do it."

"Atta girl," I said. "Let's get to it. Do you remember seeing any real campus police? Do you remember their uniforms?"

"Yeah, their shirts are blue, light blue. I guess I should have put that together right away."

"No, I don't think so. People in uniforms are intimidating. It can catch you off guard. And now you think he might be a security guard from the clinic. I think you're probably right. Do you think he might be on one of the videos you took with the body cameras?"

"Yes, I was actually reviewing some of the video yesterday. There's a lot of it. I didn't find him but there are still hours of video yet to look at."

"And now your computer and disks are gone."

189

"Yes, but don't forget, I have Canby's disks." Lindsey pulled several disks from her purse, fanning them out like a poker hand. And what about Jerry's? Do you have those?"

"I don't know. I never looked for them. I didn't know they'd be relevant until you told me about all this."

"He would have brought his laptop with him to the clinic the other night. Part of his job would be to remotely download the video from the cameras."

"There was no laptop found with him. Are you sure he would have brought it with him?"

"Absolutely. In fact he never went anywhere without it."

"Then they probably have it. Did he have copies of the disks?"

"Yes."

"Well, maybe he left them at home. I can check later. At any rate, like you said, we have Canby's. Do you know how to make more copies if we need them?"

"Yeah, sure. It's pretty easy. Why?"

"Insurance. But let's not worry about that now. Joel is our first priority. What's his last name?"

"Gibson, Joel Gibson."

"You said you think he may have been abducted by this fake cop, or security guard, or whatever he is."

"Yes."

"But you don't know for sure."

"No, not for sure."

"We have to find out. You need to call him."

"But what if…"

"It could have just been a coincidence you heard a phone ringing in the suspect's pocket when you were calling Joel. We need to be sure. If anyone other than Joel answers hand me the phone."

While she did that I checked out her bedroom. It was just as she described. I then checked each door and window. There were no signs of forced entry, which meant a key or lock picks were used. The key was unlikely so that meant lock picks.

Lindsey was clicking off her phone as I walked back into the living room.

"No answer. It went to voice mail after 5 rings. I hung up and didn't leave a message."

"Okay. His not answering means nothing. Do you know his address?"

Lindsey had Joel's address in her contacts. After she took a quick shower and changed her clothes, we headed over in the Cadillac.

On the drive over I quizzed Lindsey on Joel trying to get any information that might be helpful. She told me

Joel was from a small town in Georgia and had won an academic scholarship to the University. He never talked about his parents, but they obviously paid all his other expenses because he didn't have a part-time job like most other students. He had a roommate to share expenses and whom he complained about constantly. The roommate, Lindsey didn't know his name, was a slob and that drove Joel crazy. Joel was a neat freak. So much so Lindsey thought he must have Obsessive-Compulsive Disorder.

A few minutes later we were parked in front of Joel's building. It was another low-end row house style building in a run-down neighborhood just south of the airport.

I had Lindsey wait in the car, with the keys and motor running just in case.

I scanned the area as I walked to the building. Again, nothing looked out of place although I really didn't know what should or should not be 'in place'. I had never been in this part of town before. Walking up to the door of the apartment I noticed nothing unusual about either the door or the lockset. I stood off to the side and knocked.

There was no answer so I knocked again. There was still no answer and so I knocked a third time. I was about to walk away and check out the back door when I heard the lock being unlatched from inside.

192

"Yes? Can I help you?"

Standing in the open doorway was a man. Not a young man of college age but a middle-aged man. He looked vaguely Hispanic yet spoke with an Eastern European accent.   He was a head shorter than I was but powerfully built. His chest and shoulders stretched the fabric of his white dress shirt and his grey slacks were cinched tight around his narrow waist with a black leather belt.

"I'm looking for Joel. Joel Gibson. Is he home?"

"Joel? No he is not."

"Do you know where he is or when he'll be back?"

"Who are you? Why do you come here for Joel?"

"I'm a friend of a friend. You didn't answer my question."

"And you did not really answer my question, mister friend of a friend."

"My name is Sam Laska. And you are?"

"You are a policeman, a police officer? You act like a police officer. You ask questions in the manner of a police officer."

"I was. Not anymore. Where is Joel?"

He squared himself in the doorway and tilted his head to look over my shoulder.

"This friend of yours, it is the girl in the car across the street, yes? Why don't you both come inside? We can talk more comfortably."

"I think we're good right where we are."

"The girl is Lindsey, yes? Did Lindsey…tell you things?"

"Yes. And you're working with the fat security guard. He took Joel, didn't he? He had better be alive."

"Leon? Ha, do not worry about him. And Joel is fine. In fact he is helping me, by his own volition. He is aiding me in my work to recover property that he and others illegally obtained. He feels terrible he and the others acted so. In fact he asked me to come here and retrieve some of that property. Do you know the property which I am referring to?"

"Video and audio recordings."

"Yes."

We stood in the doorway, both of us contemplating the next move. I spoke first.

"You don't have them all."

"Yes. I know this."

"I have them. The professor's too."

"You have them here, maybe in the car with Lindsey?'

"No."

We stood staring at each other. Trying to read each other's mind.

"I think we have the basis for a bargain," he said.

"I want Joel."

"And you wish Lindsey to remain safe."

"Yes."

"When I have the remaining recordings you shall have what you want."

"And the security guard, Leon. I want him too."

"You shall have him. He is a liability now. When I have the recordings, I will tell you where Joel and Leon are. I will tell you where to leave the recordings."

"Not good. We have to do it face to face. One exchange, all at once."

"No. We shall do it as I said or not at all."

"That doesn't work for me. I think you should consult whoever is pulling your strings. I doubt he wants to see those videos played on the evening news."

Sanchez paused before he said, "I doubt very much Joel would want that to happen. You have not forgotten about him, have you?"

I felt my blood pressure rising and my jaw tighten. I wanted to smash my fist into his smug face. Instead I took a deep breath. "Call your boss," I said.

"Mr. Sam Laska, I don't believe you wish to be responsible for any tragedy that may occur if you distribute the videos. You hold a good hand but I hold all the aces. Lindsey has Joel's phone number. Call when you are ready to be reasonable." He closed the door in my face.

Back in the Cadillac I sat with my hands on the wheel and stared at Joel's door.

"Who was that guy?" Lindsey asked.

I put the car in drive and pulled away from the curb.

CHAPTER THIRTY

Sanchez watched from the front window as the Cadillac drove off. This new player in the game was a serious complication. He was no longer dealing with only young, foolish people. This man Sam Laska, who said he was once a police officer, was smart and bold. He was not intimidated by Sanchez and stood toe to toe with him. But Sanchez saw anger in his eyes. This could be an advantage for Sanchez. Angry men are rash.

Sanchez stood by the window and thumbed a number into his cell phone. Marko Rutikov answered, "Is it done?"

"No. There is a complication."

"I don't want to hear about complications. I called you to handle the complications."

"Be quiet and listen, little man. There is another. A new man we did not expect. He is helping the others. He has the remaining items."

"Who is he? How did he get...?"

197

"His name is Sam Laska. He claims he was a police officer."

"Police? The police are involved?"

"I did not say that. He said he was once a police officer. I don't know if that is true or if he said it to intimidate me. It does not seem he involved any authorities yet. I cannot be sure he will not do so soon. I need you to find out what you can about him."

"You spoke to him?"

"Yes. I offered a bargain in order to set a trap but he knew better. I cannot say for sure what he will do now. Get me the information and I will finish this. I need to know all you can learn about him."

"How can I do this? I don't..."

"You have friends. Political friends. Use them, get the favors you have paid for many times over."

"Yes. I suppose I can do that. Do we have more to go on other than the name?"

"I have a license plate number."

Sanchez gave Rutikov the number he saw on the Cadillac and clicked off his phone. He sat on a futon in the sparsely furnished living room and continued watching out the window, thinking.

Once he had the information from Rutikov he would need to act quickly. He would need to gain quick control over Sam Laska yet not harm him to the extent he would be unable to talk. He may have hidden the recordings or made copies. The optimal course of action would be to take him at this home, while he slept.

Of course, there may be others living with him. This would be fortunate. People tended to be more cooperative when their loved ones were in jeopardy. A single man could resist for quite some time, even days. But most cannot when they watch their wife or child in agony.

Maybe Lindsey would be staying with him now. Laska would naturally tell her it is not safe for her to return to her home. If she were there, Sanchez would be able to complete all his business at once.

The phone in Sanchez's pocket buzzed. It was Rutikov.

"What do you have?" Sanchez said.

"The car is registered to a Bernard Laska. I thought you said his name was Sam."

"That is what he said. It may be a relative. What is the address?"

"Eighteen-eighty four Luna Drive. That's on Siesta Key."

"I have a GPS on my car. I can find it if I need to. What else do you have?"

"Nothing right now. My people are checking that name for a driver's license or state ID card. I also have someone checking to see if he is or ever was a police officer. Do you want them to check on this Bernard Laska?"

"Yes. We may be able to use that information as well. Call me immediately when you have anything else." Sanchez clicked off his phone and stuck it back in his pocket.

Sanchez stood and scanned the street through the window. He did not like the uncertainty of the address. It would be best to know conclusively that Sam Laska lived there. Barring that, using the relative to get what he needed would have to do. It would just add more time.

Sanchez pulled his car keys from his pocket. He decided, while he was waiting for Rutikov, it was a good time to deal with the no longer useful Joel. He gathered up the computer and left through the front door.

CHAPTER THIRTY-ONE

The knuckles of my hands gripping the steering wheel had turned white. I felt the muscles in my forearms tighten. My jaw clenched and my vision was blurring. I stomped on the brake in the middle of the street and punched the dashboard. I punched it again and again until I could no longer stand the pain in my hand. My chest was tight and I was gulping air.

I sat there staring straight ahead sweat running down my face. When I caught my breath I looked over at Lindsey. She was pressed up against the passenger door, staring at me with wide eyes and an open mouth.

"Are...are you okay?" she said.

"I'm sorry. I lost it there. It happens sometimes. I've been trying to work on it."

"Yeah, well, whatever you're doing isn't working." She settled back down in the seat but kept her eyes on me. "What happened? Did that guy say something?"

"Have you ever seen him before?"

"No, who is he?"

"He's working with Leon. That's what he called the fat security guard. Although I think this guy is in charge. He's dangerous, probably much more dangerous than Leon. He said they have Joel but that Joel is helping them. He made it seem it was voluntary, that Joel wanted to help them."

"I don't believe it."

"Yeah, neither do I. He just wasn't going to admit they kidnapped him. But the guy did offer a trade, Joel and your safety for all the copies of the videos. He said they would also give us Leon to take the fall."

"Then let's do it. I want this to be over with. I want everything back to normal."

"No. It was a setup. He wanted the videos before he'd give up Joel and Leon. And a setup means they won't give up until they have the videos and there are no loose ends to worry about. That means you and me and anyone else they think knows something.

"Even if it wasn't a setup, they killed Jerry and Canby. I'm not going to let that slide. You can't either. Your life will never be the same again. Jerry is dead and his memory will always be with you. And if you just let it go you'll never have closure. You'll always blame yourself.

I'm going to finish this, Lindsey. And I need your help to do it."

Tears welled up in her eyes. "Then what about the police? Let's just call the police."

"We will, soon. I've already talked to the Detective handling Jerry's death. But when I do talk to them again, I want to hand them more. And for that I need your help."

"What do you want me to do?"

I handed her a tissue from the center counsel. "All I need is more information and for you to make copies of the disks. Those are the only copies we have and we need insurance nothing happens to them."

"I can do that. What do you need to know that I already haven't told you?"

"Tell me more about the clinic. Where is it, what's the address? What's the layout? What does it look like inside? Who's in charge, the doctor? Lets start with that."

"Well, the pain clinic is in a strip mall on the corner of Beneva and Webber. It's just a storefront. You walk into a big room that's basically the waiting room. It's set up with a bunch of folding chairs. It's always crowded. A nurse sits at a desk in the back of the room. The patients check in with her and then wait to see the doctor.

"Next to her desk is a door that leads into the back. I've never been back there but Jerry told us there are a couple of rooms off a long hallway. The doctor's office is back there."

"Okay, good. They obviously have a guard there. Does he stay out in the waiting room?"

"I think so. When I was there, I didn't really pay attention though."

"That's okay. What about the doctor? What's his name?"

"Zingara, Emile Zingara. We did research on him. He lost his license over twenty years ago after a malpractice suit. He was also convicted of writing bad script some years after losing his license. Two years ago he got his license back. Supposedly the Governor wrote a favorable letter to the Licensing Board."

"So he's the man in charge. He's the one we want."

"No, he's just an employee. The clinic is part of a chain of pain and immediate care clinics owned by The Marko Medical Group. You know, from the commercials on TV?"

"I don't think I remember seeing them."

"Come on. 'In pain? Call Marko'. You've seen those, haven't you? They're on all the time. The ads target people hurt in traffic accidents."

"I don't watch much TV. So, who owns the Marko Medical Group?"

"Dr. Marko Rutikov, but he's not a medical doctor. He's a naprapath. He's basically a glorified chiropractor. There's not much information on the Internet about how he got started and built such a big practice. He's got clinics over the entire gulf coast from Tampa down to Fort Myers and Miami too. But we figured he saw an opportunity and did a hell of a marketing job. Rutikov is a big deal in Florida and a celebrity in Sarasota. He's wealthy and donates heavily to politicians."

"So maybe he's the head of the snake. When you were doing this research, did you find out where he lives?"

"On Casey Key, the north end. He bought the whole northern tip. He had a house built there not too long ago. It was big news around here."

I sat thinking for a bit until a car behind me honked it's horn and reminded me I was blocking the street. I hit the gas, made a turn at the corner and headed south.

"What now?" Lindsey said.

"We're going to get you somewhere safe and to a computer. After that the first priority is finding Joel."

"How are you going to do that?"

"By shaking the tree. I'm going to pay a visit to the clinic."

CHAPTER THIRTY-TWO

Sanchez sat on the sofa next to the putrefying body of Leon. Joel sat weeping across from him in the wheelchair.

"Joel, I'm sorry I misled you. But you never really thought you would live through this, did you?"

"You promised," Joel said, head bowed. "You promised."

"This is necessary, my friend. No one, none of you, can be trusted to keep quiet. When I find Lindsey and her new friend they will join you. By the way, you did not tell me about him. Did you know of him, Joel?"

"New friend? I don't know what you mean."

"Sam Laska is his name. Did you know of him, Joel?"

"No. No, I don't know who that is."

"No matter. When I find them all this will be over."

Joel sniffled and looked up at Sanchez. "I can still help you. I can help you find them."

"I'm sorry, Joel. I don't really think you can." He raised the gun in his hand and placed it against Joel's forehead."

"Please. I can find Lindsey. I know where she is."

Sanchez kept the muzzle of the pistol pressed against his head. "Where, Joel? Where is she?"

"You have her computer, right? If you still have her computer, I can track her phone."

"How?"

"Through an app, an application. It's called 'Find My Phone'. Most everyone I know uses it. You link your phone and computer and if you ever lose your phone or it gets stolen you can find out where it is. As long as the phone is turned on, you can find it."

"This application gives you an address?"

"No, it displays a map and shows you where the phone is on the map."

"Show me, Joel."

Sanchez retrieved Lindsey's computer, cut the duct tape binding Joel's arms to the wheelchair, and handed the laptop to him. After a few moments the computer booted up and Joel began tapping away on the keyboard.

"Here, see? See this? See the red dot on the map? That's where her phone is. That's where she is."

Sanchez leaned over Joel and studied the map displayed on the screen. All the streets were marked clearly and individual buildings were outlined. A flashing icon in the shape of an inverted teardrop marked the phone's location in a large building."

"Where is that? What is that place?"

Joel zoomed in on the icon.

"The hospital, Sarasota Memorial Hospital."

Sanchez stood upright. "Why is she at the hospital?" Sanchez said, more to himself than Joel.

"I don't know. Maybe she's hurt or sick or something."

"And what happens when she moves? The map will change, yes?"

"Yes, it will always track the phone's location. You can follow it anywhere as long as you have a wifi connection to the computer."

"How do I do this if I am in my car?"

"Turn your phone's hotspot on. You have a smartphone, right? That's what I just did. I have Lindsey's computer connected to the wifi hotspot of my phone."

"Your phone and this computer are already connected? Thank you, Joel."

Sanchez shot Joel in the back of the head splattering his brains over Leon's dead body.

CHAPTER THIRTY-THREE

I took Lindsey to the morgue at Sarasota Memorial to see Marley.

"What are we doing here?" Lindsey said as I parked the car in the high-rise lot across Waldemere Street.

"I have a friend who works here. I'm hoping she'll let us use her computer and let you stay at her place for a few hours. At least until I get back from the clinic. After that I'll take you over to my dad's house on Siesta Key. You'll be able to stay there until all this is over."

"When will that be?"

"Very soon, I hope."

We made our way through the pedestrian walkway that connected the hospital to the garage and made our way through the maze of hallways. As we got close I could see Lindsey make a face and hold her nose.

"Ugh. What's that smell?"

"The morgue. My friend works in the morgue."

211

"Can I wait outside? I don't think I want to go in there."

"Don't worry. You won't see anything. There's an anteroom, a reception area we'll be in."

We pushed through the swinging doors. No one was around.

"My friend must be in back," I said. I could see Lindsey was still holding her nose and now looked a little pale. "Why don't you sit down over there?" I pointed to a row of chairs against the back wall. "I'll go find my friend."

As I walked to the counter Marley came through the swinging stainless steel doors that led to the post room. She smiled when she saw me.

"Hi, I was hoping I'd see you soon. I'll be leaving in about an hour. And my uncle wants you to call him. Here's his number." She handed me the business card of Detective Nosmo King. "I wrote his cellphone number on the back."

"Yeah, I need to talk to him too. But I need to talk to you first." As I said this, I saw Marley look over my shoulder to Lindsey.

"That's Lindsey, Jerry's girlfriend. I found her this morning after I left your place. We need a favor."

212

I filled Marley in on everything that happened since she left her apartment. I told her about finding Lindsey and how all this started with the Manasota Pain Management Clinic and Marko Rutikov. I told her about Canby's ambitions, Leon the security guard, Joel, the videos, and the new player who offered me a trade for Joel and Leon.

"My God, you were right. Jerry was murdered. Do you really think Rutikov is involved? Do you think he knows what's going on at that clinic?"

"I don't know. The doctor there, Zingara, might have seen an opportunity to make some money and started a side business using the clinic. It is possible Rutikov is so far removed from the day-to-day operations of every clinic he owns that he wouldn't know. I plan to find out though."

"And what about Joel? Are you going to make the trade? The police need to know, Sam."

"What was offered was a trap, not a legit trade. I have an idea about how to find where Joel is. When I do I'll call Nosmo, I promise. First, I want to make insurance copies of the disks Lindsey has but I don't have a computer. I was hoping we could use yours, your laptop back at home."

"Yeah, sure. But I don't have a burner on it."

"A what?"

"A DVD burner, a device that copies the disks. It wasn't standard on my laptop."

"We don't need one," Lindsey said from the back of the room. Her elbows were on her knees and her hands cradled the sides of her head. She looked even more pale than she had when she first sat down. "I can just copy them to the Cloud. I can get an account for free." She stood and braced herself against the back of her chair. "Can I wait downstairs? I think I'm gonna be sick if I stay here much longer."

"Go ahead. I'll meet you in the lobby but don't wander off. I mean it," I said.

"Don't worry, you're my White Knight." She managed a weak smile and hurried through the doors into the hallway.

I turned back to Marley. "What's the Cloud?"

"Basically it's cyberspace. You get an account with a company and you can upload files to their servers, which are located who knows where. They store all your stuff indefinitely and many of them are free. Your account is password protected and available to you from any computer in the world as long as you're connected to the Internet."

"So we don't need to make new disks?"

"No. You can even give a temporary password for your account to anyone if you want to share the files."

"Wow, I really gotta learn about this stuff."

"Start with getting your own phone first." She smiled at me again.

"Yeah, as soon as I can. So, can we use your laptop?"

"Of course. Like I said, I'll be leaving here in about an hour. Wait for me there?"

"I have something to do first and I want to meet with Nosmo. Is it okay to leave Lindsey there until I get back?"

"Yes, and when I get there I can stay with her until you get back."

"Thank you. I'll hurry," I said. I turned and headed to the door.

"Sam," Marley said as I pushed open the door, "Be careful."

"I will," I said as I left.

CHAPTER THIRTY-FOUR

When I got down to the main floor of the hospital, I headed to the lobby to meet up with Lindsey. The lobby wasn't very large. It was only a seating area dotted with chairs and magazine covered side tables. There was also a kiosk shop that sold coffee and other snacks set off to the side. The outside wall was floor to ceiling glass that looked out over a small concrete veranda adjacent to the entry doors. The veranda was furnished with steel chairs and benches.

Barely half the seats in the lobby and on the veranda were occupied. Lindsey wasn't there. Standing in the middle of the lobby I could see up and down the three hallways that intersected and met at the lobby. I scanned the faces trying to pick her out in the thin crowd of senior citizens, lab coats, and scrub-clad employees. She wasn't there. I felt a drop of sweat roll down the center of my back.

I stood there looking up and down the halls at the streams of people and thinking. There would be no sense in her leaving without me. Even if she panicked and decided to bolt she had no ride and nowhere to go. And it wasn't possible that she was taken. There was no way we could have been followed. Or maybe there was. I didn't really check my back when we left Joel's apartment. I was too pissed off and didn't even think to check.

"Hey, there you are." It was Lindsey, coming down the hall past the coffee kiosk.

"Where the hell were you? I was getting worried."

"I was in the bathroom. That smell made me sick, I threw up a little. I'm okay now."

"Yeah, okay. I should have guessed. From now on and until this is over I need to know where you are at all times. Got it?"

"Sure, I get it. I thought I'd be back before you came back downstairs."

"Yeah, okay. Come on, lets get out of here. We're going to Marley's place. It's not far from here. You can use her computer and copy those videos."

Fifteen minutes later we were inside Marley's apartment. We found her laptop on a desk in the bedroom and Lindsey booted it up. On the Internet she went to a site named 'Nimbus" and started an application for a free account.

"Put it in my name," I said.

"Sure, no problem. Any reason why?"

"I want you out of this. When you finish copying the disks, I want you to destroy them. Erase them, break them, burn them, whatever. Just destroy them."

"Okay. Do you want the account password protected?"

"Yeah, but I don't want you to know it."

When the box popped up asking for a password, Lindsey stepped away and I entered my new password and Lindsey went to work copying the files. I watched as she inserted the first disk and began uploading it to my new Cloud account. A little blue bar showed the progress of the upload.

"It's moving pretty slowly, isn't it?" I said.

"Yeah, there's a lot of data on each disk."

After fifteen minutes the upload was complete and she popped out the disk. "Only four more to go," she said.

"I'm going to go now. Make sure you destroy the disks when you're done."

I told her I was going to the clinic and I'd be back as soon as I could. Until then she was to lock the doors behind me and she was not to let anyone in other than

218

Marley or myself. I would keep Marley's key but I'd knock when I came back.

As I walked to the Cadillac, Jerry's cellphone buzzed in my pocket. The banner across the top said 'Home', Josie's house. I pushed the button to answer and heard my Dad's voice.

"Sam?"

"Yeah, Dad."

"You didn't forget about me dropping off Josie's car did you? I'm gonna need that ride soon."

"Dad, something came up. I can't do it."

"What? Dammit, Sam! I told you…"

"Dad, hang on. Let me explain," and I did. As I stood on the sidewalk in front of Marley's building I gave him a quickie run down of everything that had happened today.

"Jesus, Sam. What now?"

"I'm going to shake things up and stop at the pain clinic. But I just had an idea. Can you run home to your place and then meet me?"

"Yeah. What do you need?"

I told Dad what I wanted and to wait for me in the north end of the shopping center parking lot at Tamiami and Siesta Drive. When I got what I wanted at the clinic I would call Nosmo King to meet me there too.

CHAPTER THIRTY-FIVE

I pulled into the lot at Beneva and Webber and backed the Cadillac into a spot opposite the front entrance of the clinic. It was a storefront located on the short side of an 'L' shaped strip mall with a brick façade and a glass door. Steel security gates were folded to the side of the door. The name, Manasota Pain Management Clinic, was painted on the glass door. A cardboard sign hung below the name displaying the hours of operation.

There were few other cars in the lot but as I walked in, I had to jostle my way through a crowd of people to get near the nurse's desk. Most of the people waiting were young, probably in their early thirties or younger. None wore a pained expression of chronic suffering on their faces common to the diseased or injured. Aside from looking pale and drawn most looked healthy.

I moved in front of the nurse's desk. She didn't bother looking up at me before she said, "Take a number, you'll be called in order." She lifted her arm and motioned to a stand with a stack of numbers hanging from a hook.

"I'm not a patient. I'm looking for Leon."

The security guard, who had been leaning back against a wall next to the nurse, straightened up. I looked him up and down. He was a scrawny kid, though taller than me, about twenty-five years old. He wore black pants and a baggy white uniform shirt that hung off of him. Pinned to the shirt was a cheap gold badge that read 'Security'. He had no gun, only a can of pepper spray and a low-budget Taser hooked on his belt.

The nurse looked up at me. "And who are you?" She said.

"Sam Laska. Where is Leon, the other security guard?"

"I'm sorry, there is no Leon that works here."

The guard edged a little closer.

"That doesn't work for me," I said and moved around to the back of the desk. The nurse began to stand. I put a hand on her shoulder and pushed her back down into her chair. The scrawny guard came around the desk at me while fumbling for his Taser. I moved at him quicker and thrust out my left arm, hitting him in the chest with the heel of my hand. As he fell back, I grabbed the hand that was reaching for the Taser and applied a wristlock, twisting

221

the joint against its natural rotation. I slipped the Taser
from its holster and guided the kid to the floor.

"Stay there or I'll break your arm next time," I
said. I turned back to the nurse who was staring at me with
an open mouth. "I'm going to ask you one more time,
nicely. Where is Leon?"

"I...I don't know. He hasn't been in for a few
days. That's why Timmy is here."
She glanced over to the kid on the floor and back to me.

I heard the door open and a rustle of footsteps
behind me. The waiting room was clearing out.

"Where does he live?"

"I don't know. Dr. Zingara keeps the employee
records back in his office."

I looked around the now empty room. There were
no phones anywhere in the place.

"Give me your cellphones," I said.

"What?" she said.

"Give me your cellphones. I'll bet you both have a
cellphone. Hand them over. Don't make me search you
for them."

The kid on the floor quickly dug his out of a front
pocket of his pants and tossed it to me. The nurse said
hers was in her purse under her desk. I let her take it out
while I watched her. She handed it to me.

"You'll get these back when I leave here," I said. I put both phones in my back pocket and stuck the Taser in my belt. I pushed through a cheap wooden door behind the nurse's desk and stepped into a long hallway that ran the width of the building. To my left and almost directly in front of me was another cheap door. Taped to the door was a sheet of notebook paper with the words 'Exam Room' handwritten on it.

I shoved the door open and walked in. Seated on a paper covered steel exam table was a naked girl. She couldn't have been more than seventeen. Standing, facing her was a thin, wrinkled, bald man in a grey lab coat. He turned quickly and took a step away from the girl as I entered. The girl moved only enough to turn her head and look at me with glassy eyes.

"What is this?" he said. "I'm examining a patient. Get out."

I grabbed Dr. Zingara by the collar and pushed him into to a chair next to a desk at the back of the room. "If you move or say anything, I'll snap your neck." I turned to the girl. "Put on your clothes and get out." She stared at me through dead eyes for a long moment and gathered her clothes. Still naked, she shuffled from the room. I closed the door behind her and turned back to Zingara.

"I was…I was examining her. She has…"

"I know what you were doing. Now shut up and listen." I stood over him and leaned in close. "My name is Laska, Sam Laska. Say it."

"What?"

"Say my name. Say 'Sam Laska'."

"Sam Laska." I could barely hear him.

"Say it again. Louder."

"Sam Laska."

"When I leave here you're going to call Rutikov and tell him my name. Do you understand?"

"Yes."

"Now, where are the employee records?"

"There," he pointed to a filing cabinet. "In that cabinet, the top drawer."

I pulled open the drawer and flipped through a small stack of manila files. I found one marked 'Irsay, Leon' on the tab and pulled it out.

"Leon Irsay, is he the security guard?"

"Yes, but he's not here."

I ignored Zingara and flipped through the file. It listed only the basics: his name, birthdate, social security number, address and phone number. It had a short description of an auto, a 1991 Chevy Camaro, and a Polaroid photo of Leon wearing his uniform.

I stuck the file under my arm and turned back to Zingara. "Who's the Hispanic-looking guy? The one with the Russian accent."

"I don't know. I don't know who you're talking about."

I took a step closer. "Who is he?"

Zingara sunk deeper into his seat. "I don't know. I swear I don't know."

I tossed the cellphones and Taser onto the desk and turned away. "Call Rutikov," I said as I left.

CHAPTER THIRTY-SIX

Sanchez drove to the hospital. He checked the laptop and the inverted teardrop as often as he could. Rush hour was beginning and traffic was heavy. The drive would take longer than he anticipated. He slipped between the cars as quickly as he could but only made small gains. Two miles from the hospital traffic came to a standstill.

He checked the laptop. The teardrop had moved. It was no longer hovering over the hospital. He watched it for movement as traffic began moving again. The teardrop hovered over a building less than a mile from the hospital. It had stopped.

Sanchez maneuvered the car through the traffic and drove towards the teardrop. As he finally drew near he saw a man standing on the sidewalk. Sam Laska was talking on a cellphone. Sanchez pulled to the curb at a safe distance and watched as Laska finished his call and drove away in the Cadillac. The laptop showed the teardrop still

226

hovering over the building Laska had been standing in front of. Lindsey was inside.

But which apartment was she in? The two-story building had open walkways exposing each apartment's door to the street. There were many doors and Sanchez had no way of knowing which was the right one. He could not risk being seen while checking each doorbell. He would have to wait until Laska came back. He opened his window, cut the engine, and settled in to wait.

I pulled into the shopping mall's parking lot and drove to the north end. Josie's Infinity was parked in a spot and Dad was standing outside, leaning against the car. I pulled in next to him. As I got out of the Cadillac, Dad leaned into the Infinity through the open driver's side window. He came out holding a small black plastic case and handed it to me.

"Thanks, Dad," I said. I opened the case and examined the matte black Glock 9mm pistol protected in foam rubber padding. A fully loaded magazine was nestled next to it.

"What are you gonna do now, Sam?"

"First I'm calling Detective King and then I'm going over to Leon Irsay's house."

"Who's that again?"

"He's the security guard, the one that dumped Jerry's body and probably the one who killed him."

I grabbed Leon's file and switched cars with Dad. The new guy had seen the Cadillac and I wanted to get as close as I could without being made. I got into the Infinity and took my Glock from its case. I loaded the magazine and worked the slide to chamber a round. I tucked the pistol into the back of my pants and started the car.

I took out Jerry's phone and dialed the number for Nosmo that Marley gave me. He answered on the second ring.

"Detective King."

"Nosmo, it's Sam."

"Yeah, good. You got my message. We found Captain Bob. He's sitting here in an interview room but refuses to say anything. He says he wants to talk to the guy in the Cadillac. That's you I'm guessing."

"Yeah, that's me. But something more important has come up." I was getting tired of explaining everything that happened today. First Marley then Dad and now Nosmo. But if anyone needed to know it was Nosmo. I gave him the short version and told him I'd fill in the blanks and answer any questions when I saw him.

"Meet me at the security guards house," I said. "How fast can you get there?"

"Sam, I think we've got enough for a Search Warrant. That's the way to go. You're talking multiple murders here. I don't want to lose this in court because of a bad search."

"I can't do that, Nosmo. The kid, Joel, is probably there. We have to get to him before they decide they don't need him any longer."

"But we don't know for sure that he's there."

"No, but it's a good bet he is."

"You know I can't go in without a warrant, Sam. If I knock and he turns me away, all we're doing is showing our hand."

"They already know that I know where Leon lives. We have to get there before they move him or worse. How about this? I'm not law enforcement anymore. I'm a private citizen. I don't need a warrant. If I go in and see evidence of a crime and someone who is in imminent danger and report it you can enter without a warrant."

"Yeah, that's true. There's no violation there."

"So we have a plan. You hang back, across the street or down the block, and if I see something I'll give you the high sign."

"What's the address?" Nosmo said.

CHAPTER THIRTY-SEVEN

Sanchez continued to watch for Laska's return. He was content to wait. He had a good view of the front of the building and every door and would see if Lindsey tried to leave that way. If she tried to leave through the back he would see the teardrop move.

A phone buzzed. He glanced at both Joel's phone next to the laptop and then at his lying on the center counsel. It was his phone. Rutikov was calling.

He pushed the green button on the screen to answer. "Sanchez," he said into the phone.

"It's Rutikov."

"Yes, I know that. Did you get more information?"

"Yes, but that's not why I'm calling. This Sam Laska, he knows about the clinic. He went there. He assaulted my people. He took Irsay's file. How did he find out about him? He knows where Irsay lives."

231

"Of course he knows about the clinic. He was with the girl, Lindsey. He has the videos. And I gave him Leon's name. It does not matter."

"What are you talking about? Why would you give him Leon's name? My God, this is all falling apart."

"Calm down. I am handling this. If he goes to Leon's house, he will understand the urgency of turning over the videos. I have found the girl and I am waiting for Laska. He will give me the videos. And soon after that they will be dead."

Sanchez continued to watch the building as he talked with Rutikov. He saw the pretty girl dressed in hospital scrubs walking down the street. She turned into the small courtyard of the building and took the stairs to the second floor.

"What else did you find out about Laska?" Sanchez said.

"He never was a police officer, at least not in Florida. He does have a Florida Driver's License. He only got it a few months ago. It was a transfer from Illinois. My people are checking to see if he was ever a police officer there. That will take a while longer."

The girl in the scrubs stopped in front of a door at the corner of the building. She tried the door but it was locked. She knocked. Lindsey opened the door.

"It is no longer important," Sanchez said.

I drove down the block and found Leon's house. It was a small, depressing single story cinder block house with an attached garage. The front yard was littered with debris and overgrown with weeds. I drove past quickly and turned to circle the block. I didn't want to chance Leon making me. When I came around to his street again I found a spot far enough away to watch the house yet not be seen. I parked and waited for Nosmo.

A few minutes later he pulled behind the Infinity in a black Crown Vic. I walked over and got in the passenger's seat.

"I half expected you to bring the cavalry along," I said.

"I thought about it but figured it would look like we set this up. So here I am. Your only backup."

"I get the feeling you can handle it."

"Let's hope you don't need more. You carrying?"

I slipped my Glock from the small of my back, showed it to Nosmo, then tucked it into the front of my pants. I covered it with my shirt.

We got out of the Crown Vic and Nosmo waited while I approached the house. As I stepped up to the front door I got a hint of a familiar odor. I looked back towards Nosmo. We had a clear view of each other. I knocked but guessed there would be no response. I was right so I tried the door. It was locked. The odor was enough for me so I kicked in the door. I saw the two bodies and signaled Nosmo to hurry over.

I waited for him before entering the room. Nosmo got a whiff of the rotting body on the couch and covered his nose and mouth with a frayed handkerchief he pulled from his back pocket. We stepped into the house being careful not to disturb anything.

The body on the couch was Leon. His bloated face was still recognizable. The boy seated in a wheelchair facing Leon I guessed was Joel. His feet were bound to the chair by duct tape wrapped around his ankles. His hands were free but had been bound the same way. Pieces of duct tape were still stuck to the arms of the wheelchair.

"Sweet Jesus," Nosmo said.

"Yeah, sweet Jesus is right. That's Leon over there," I said. "And this kid must be Joel." I held the back of my hand to Joel's cheek. "I would think Leon's been dead two or more days but Joel can't be more than a couple of hours. The body hasn't cooled very much yet."

I took a step back and scanned the room. I was going into full-on Homicide Detective mode. I took in the entire room noticing all the major and minor details at once. I noted the placement of the bodies and their wounds, the furniture, the doors and windows, and the blood spatter. I saw glasses and beer cans on side tables, bullet casings on the floor, discarded sections of a newspaper in a corner, and even dust voids on the desk where objects had been removed. I wanted to get to work but this was not my job.

Nosmo, still holding the handkerchief over his nose and mouth, was crouched next to Joel. He was checking out the wounds in the back and front of his head. "Looks like a single through and through. Entered the back and out the front," he said.

I stepped closer. "The hair is singed around the entrance wound. And there's stippling. The weapon was close, less than six inches. Looks like a downward trajectory too," I said. I looked at the undamaged wall behind Leon. "I'll bet the round is in Leon."

Nosmo stood up. "I'll bet you're right," he said. He began looking around the room. "I gotta call this in." He pulled his cellphone from his pocket.

"We should search the rest of the house first. Someone could still be here. Or worse, another body."

235

Nosmo pulled a pair of surgical gloves from his sport coat pocket and handed them to me. He pulled out a second pair for himself. After pulling them on we went through the rest of the house. We moved through the place like we were long-time partners alternately covering each other while the other opened doors or checked around corners. We found nothing until we came to the garage.

The Chevy Camaro was parked facing the overhead door. I noticed the damage to the front first.

"Nosmo, take a look at this," I said. "This looks recent."

Nosmo came around and stood next to me. He crouched down to take a closer look. "Sure does. I'll bet you're right. I'll bet that professor was killed by this car."

"It shouldn't be hard to match up."

"Yeah, there was debris from the striking vehicle in the lot and paint scrapings on another car that was hit."

Nosmo stood and pulled his cellphone out. "I'm calling this in now. We need to wait outside until the Criminalistics Unit gets here. My Sergeant will be coming out and I'd bet some of the brass too. We don't get double homicides too often."

We headed out the way we came in. In the front yard, I pulled off my gloves and stood nearby as Nosmo made his call. I was still thinking like a homicide detective. I was organizing a to-do list in my head. First there would be a walk-through, taking rough notes and a quick sketch of the scene. Then the Criminalists take over. They'd photo and video the scene, take measurements, and begin to collect evidence. They would dust for prints. There would be bullet trajectories to determine and blood spatter patterns to analyze. After the ME's office gave the okay the bodies and wounds would be examined and photographed. The neighborhood would be canvassed to learn if anyone saw or heard anything. There would be hours and hours of work ahead for Nosmo and the others. I envied them.

The Medical Examiner's office, I thought. Marley. I should call Marley and check on Lindsey. Before I could get Jerry's phone out of my pocket it buzzed. The screen told me Lindsey was calling.

"Lindsey," I said into the phone.

"No, Sam Laska. I am not Lindsey," the voice said in a Russian accent.

I felt like a bomb had gone off in my head. I broke out in a cold sweat and every muscle in my body went taut. I thought I might vomit. This son of a bitch had Lindsey.

How did he find her? I wasn't followed. I made sure of it, carefully checking my mirrors as I drove her to Marley's house.

"Do you understand I am calling you on Lindsey's phone?" he said.

Through clenched teeth I answered, "Yes. She had better be alive."

"Of course. Why would you think otherwise?"

"You killed Joel. You didn't have to kill him."

"Good, you found him, and Leon too. I was hoping you would. Now you understand how serious I am."

"I understand. I don't think you understand how serious I am."

"Yes, yes. Of course you are."

"What do you want?"

"You are a smart man, Sam Laska. You had Lindsey copy the files and destroy the disks. I have the broken disks. Now I need the password."

"And then you'll kill Lindsey just like you killed Joel."

"No, Sam Laska. I will give her to you if you give me the password."

"I don't believe you."

"Then come here. You know where we are. You type in the password and you can have her."

"I'll be there."

"You have only twenty minutes. And you know not to bring the police. People will die if you bring the police."

"I understand."

"And Sam Laska, I have your friend Marley Jones too. Twenty minutes and then I flip a coin. Who will I hurt first, Sam Laska?"

The line went dead. I stood there with Jerry's phone in my hand and staring into space. The rage inside of me was growing. My heart was pounding and the pressure was building. My head throbbed with pain. I tried to push it aside and think clearly. I was afraid I wouldn't be able to do it.

Nosmo had finished his call and walked over to me. "You okay? You're red as a beet," he said.

"That was him, he has Marley. And Lindsey too. He wants me there to give him the password for the files."

"Jesus, Marley! How…?"

"I don't know. I have to go." I pulled out the keys to the Infinity and ran to the car. Nosmo ran with me, huffing and puffing all the way.

"I'm going too," he said.

We stood next to the Infinity. "No. He said I had to come alone. We can't risk it."

"She's my niece, Sam. She's like my daughter. You aren't going to stop me."

I knew I wasn't going to win the argument. "Get in," I said.

I started the car and looked back at Leon's house before I pulled away. "What about the scene? You're people are on the way."

"Fuck it. Those bodies aren't going anywhere. Drive."

I raced to Marley's house, dodging traffic and blowing through stoplights and signs. We barely had fifteen minutes left to get there. Nosmo called out short cuts through the neighborhoods and watched for cross traffic at the intersections. We were getting close.

"You know it's a setup, Sam."

"Yeah, but what choice do I have?"

"You can't go in with your gun blazing. He'll kill you, Marley, and Lindsey."

"I know."

"Then what's the plan?"

"I'm going to trade myself for Marley and Lindsey. I have the password, he doesn't need them."

"Yes he does. There's no reason for you to give him the password without leverage."

"You got another idea?"

"He doesn't know about me coming along. We have to use that."

"How about this then?" And I told Nosmo the only other thing I could think of.

CHAPTER THIRTY-EIGHT

I ran up the stairs to Marley's apartment taking them two at a time. I was alone. I had dropped Nosmo off around the back and down the street. He would make his way to the backstairs and come into Marley's bedroom through the window. A window I forgot to close when I left this morning. I would stall the Russian as long as I could, then get him into the bedroom where Marley's computer was. I hoped the girls weren't being held there. Nosmo would have surprise on his side and we should be able to take the Russian together, away from the girls.

I knocked on the door.

"Come in," the Russian said from inside.

I drew a deep breath and opened the door and went in. Marley and Lindsey were seated next to one another on the sofa. Their hands and feet were bound with electrical cord probably torn from Marley's lamps. They were gagged with strips of a torn bed sheet. The same

242

sheet Marley and I had made love on what seemed to be an eternity ago.

The Russian was standing in front of them, a pistol in his right hand. With his left he held up a coin.

"You had only seconds to spare, Sam Laska," he said.

"You son of a bitch," I said.

"Yes, I am that. My father was Soviet military and my mother was a Cuban whore."

"Let me guess, he was assigned there. But he went back after the USSR broke up."

"Yes, he went back to his wife and child. But I found them. I went to Russia and found him and his family."

"And he rejected you."

"No, he embraced me. He took me in. His wife had died and I lived with him and his son, my half-brother. He taught me many things."

"Your half-brother? Rutikov. Rutikov is your half-brother."

"Yes. Now you see, don't you Sam Laska?"

I took a half step forward, trying to edge closer. The Russian raised his gun and pointed it at Marley. I saw the fear in her eyes. I stopped.

"Are you armed, Sam Laska?" he said.

"Just call me Sam," I said. "And what do I call you?"

"Sanchez will do. It is my mother's name. Again, are you carrying a weapon?"

"No." I held up my hands and did a three-sixty turn.

"Raise your shirt, Sam."

I did. The Glock was still tucked safely in the front of my pants.

"You lied to me, Sam. Carefully remove the gun, place it on the floor, and kick it towards me."

I did as I was told. "Did you really expect me to tell you about the gun?" I said.

"I would have been disappointed if you did," he said.

"What now?"

"You give me the password and I will leave you and your friends."

"How can I trust you'll honor your word and let us go? You'll know you have the right password. I expect you'll want to watch me type it in. But once you have it I have no leverage."

"Then we are at a standoff. You will need to trust me if you wish me to leave here."

I stood staring at him. I wanted him to think I was deciding my options.

Sanchez spoke first. "Come now, Sam. You know you have no choice."

I sighed. I hoped it didn't look too faked. "Okay, let's go to the computer and you can watch me type in the password.

Sanchez looked down at Marley and Lindsey on the sofa. "I believe I bound you securely. Still, do not try anything or I will hurt Sam."

Sanchez stepped closer to me. He now held his gun on me. "Let's do this now. You will lead the way, Sam," he said.

A loud ringing came from the bedroom. A cellphone, Nosmo's cellphone, played the theme from a cop reality show. Sanchez turned to the sound.

Nothing ever goes the way you hope. You try to anticipate every glitch or problem but it just isn't possible. If we had weeks or months to plan we might be able to put the odds in our favor. We had only minutes and those minutes weren't good enough. Nosmo was found out and soon Sanchez would have all four of us.

Partners, police partners, always have this conversation. The bad guy gets the drop on one of them and gets his gun. He demands the other's gun or he'll shoot his partner. What does the other partner do? His partner is a hostage and might be killed. But if he gives up his gun they might both be killed. My rule, most cops' rule, is never give up your gun. One might die but never both. I wasn't going to force Nosmo to make that decision. Not with four lives, one of them his niece, at stake.

I grabbed at Sanchez's gun with my left hand. I turned into him, my back to him as if we were spooning. I gripped the gun with both hands now, fighting for control. Sanchez twisted to his right, trying to face me again, and hit me in the jaw with a left cross. He was strong and it dazed me but I hung on to the pistol with both hands. He was trying to turn the business end of it towards me. I bent over and bit his hand. There are no rules in a death match.

He screamed and let go of the gun. I spit out a chunk of flesh. He hit me again, another left to the jaw and then a right with his wounded hand. The punch stunned me and I staggered back, dropping the gun. He dove to the floor, snatched up the gun, and turned it towards me. Three shots rang out.

Nosmo stood in the doorway to the dining room, a wisp of smoke rising from the gun in his hand. Sanchez laid dead, three small blooms of red spreading across his white shirt.

Nosmo went to Sanchez and kicked the gun from his hand and checked for a pulse. I went to Marley and Lindsey, pulled off their gags and began untying them. Marley threw her arms around me. We both held on, afraid to let go.

CHAPTER THIRTY-NINE

It was a long night for us all, more so for Nosmo and the Sarasota Police Department. Processing of the two scenes, Leon's house and Marley's apartment, wasn't completed until the next morning. The interviews lasted almost as long. Lindsey and I took the longest. Sanchez had told Lindsey and Marley he tracked Lindsey's cellphone using Lindsey's computer. He laughed when he explained Joel showed him how to do it.

Marley's interview was quicker. And Captain Bob, we learned his last name was Quinn, opened up after I talked to him. He told his story just as he had told me days earlier.

The media were all over. The local stations were broadcasting live from the scenes and Police Headquarters. The newspaper had people at all three places as well. Nosmo told me Dr. Zingara and his nurse had both been arrested and the Florida Department of Law Enforcement

248

was being called in. They would investigate Rutikov's other clinics.

"And what about him?" I asked Nosmo.

"There are no plans to bring him in yet. He's a powerful man in the State. We can't prove he's involved yet so until we get more we can't move on him. We need to have a dead bang case. He'll march in here with an army of attorneys and walk right out if we don't."

"What about Zingara or the nurse? Are they talking yet?"

"No, but it's only a matter of time. When they see they're facing big jail time they'll talk."

"I hope so."

Nosmo wasn't nearly done yet. So I took Marley to her place to pick up a change of clothes and some personal items. Marley's apartment hadn't been released yet so Nosmo called ahead and let the officers still on the scene know we were coming. She would stay with me at Dad's house. I called Dad and let him know. And I told him to let Josie know it was all over. I didn't want her to see it on television.

Marley and I finally got to bed about ten in the morning. We were too tired, physically and emotionally, to make love. We fell asleep holding each other close.

Marko Rutikov had watched the news reports all night. His brother was dead. The police had the video files and Zingara and his nurse were under arrest. One news station was reporting they had unconfirmed information the FDLE was beginning an investigation into Rutikov's clinics. His world was falling apart.

Zingara would surely talk. He would put it all off on Rutikov to save his own skin. Then the other Doctors in all the other clinics would fall like dominos. They would all blame Marko Rutikov. He needed to call his attorney. But his attorney would tell him to turn himself in. His attorney would delay and delay and use the tricks and traps and loopholes in the law to drag this out for years. It would cost Rutikov millions. And in the end he would be broke and may still go to prison.

He would call the Governor. The Governor had just as much at stake as did he. He took out his cellphone and hit the Governor's private number on speed dial.

The phone rang four times before Governor Thomas Henderson picked up.

"Hello, Marko," he said.

"Can you talk?" Rutikov said.

"Yes, I'm alone. Just doing some paperwork. What can I do for you?"

"Have you heard? Do you know what's happening?"

"Yes, Marko. It hasn't hit the news in Tallahassee yet but I have people throughout the State who keep me informed."

"You have to stop this. They say the FDLE is getting involved. Call them off, Thomas."

"I can't do that, Marko. I don't have that kind of power. What about your lawyers? What are they doing? What do they say?"

"Fuck the lawyers. I want this ended now. You can do it. You're the Governor for God's sake."

"This isn't Russia, Marko. I can't be involved. I can't be seen as trying to influence the investigation in any way. The press would hear about it. It would ruin my career."

"You're abandoning me? Do you think you can do that? Do I have to remind you that you are involved in this?"

"Marko, you know that's not true. I had no idea what was going on in those clinics."

"You knew, Thomas. You knew very well. And if this doesn't end now it will be the end of you. You will end up in prison with me."

"Are you threatening me?"

"Yes. Yes I am. You end this now."

Marko Rutikov listened to silence on the other end of the line. The Governor spoke again.

"Okay, Marko. I will end this. But it will take some time. You need to leave the country for awhile."

"How long?"

"Not long. I'm going to send one of my people to you. He will stay with you until we can get you out. I'm sending him to you in my jet. He'll be there tonight."

"And you'll fix this? You'll have them call off the investigation?"

"Yes, Marko."

"Good, I'll start packing. You had better come through, Thomas."

"Don't worry, Marko. I'll make sure you never spend a day in jail."

CHAPTER FORTY

Jerry's Memorial Service was that afternoon. After oversleeping, Marley and I rushed to shower and dress. We arrived just as the service started. Lindsey was there and Josie insisted she sit with her. Other classmates of Jerry's were there as well. Nosmo showed up wearing the same sad sport coat he had on yesterday. He hadn't been home yet.

After the service we talked with Josie and extended our condolences. I introduced Marley to Josie and my father. As I expected, my father barely spoke to Marley and seemed uncomfortable being near her. Josie took Marley's hand and treated her like she was her own family. She led Marley to a sofa and they sat talking alone.

My father stepped towards me. "Sam…" he said. But I turned and walked away to talk to Nosmo.

He told me some preliminary findings came back. The shell casings recovered in Leon's house matched Sanchez's pistol. The bullets, buried in Leon's body, would

253

take longer as his body was awaiting autopsy. Sanchez's fingerprints were also all over Leon's house.

During their search the Criminalists found three laptops in a car registered to Sanchez. They also found more DVDs in the car and a melted lump of plastic in the trash. Nosmo figured they were Jerry's copies of the videos.

"What about Zingara and the nurse? Have they given up Rutikov yet?" I said.

"The nurse is hanging tough. She asked for a lawyer. Zingara is starting to crack though. He wants to know what he'll be offered before he says anything. The State Attorney's office was called and they're trying to work something out. It won't be much longer."

Josie was hosting a luncheon after the service but Marley and I begged off. We went back to Dad's house. We undressed and made love in my bed. Afterward, as we lay holding one another, Marley whispered in my ear.

"Thank you. Thank you for saving me."

"Don't say that. It's my fault. I never should have involved you. I should have brought Lindsey here instead. I never should have put you in danger like that. I'm so sorry."

"No, there's no way you could have known. Don't blame yourself."

"Still," I said. "I'm sorry. I'm so sorry."

We lay there quiet, still holding each other. When I was sure she was asleep, I crept out of bed and dressed in the dark. I tucked my pistol into the back of my pants and drove away in Josie's Infinity.

I crossed the South Bridge onto the mainland and turned south on Tamiami. A few miles later I made a right turn and crossed the Intracoastal Waterway onto Casey Key. I found Marko Rutikov's estate on the far north end of the key. It was surrounded by an eight-foot high stone wall and an iron gate across the entrance. The gate was open.

I drove through and up the winding driveway to the house. I parked behind a black SUV, a rental, near the front entrance and walked around to the back of the house. I stepped over a pillared concrete fence and onto a marble patio. Rutikov was sitting on a lounge chair looking out into what is the black void of the Gulf of Mexico at night. He had a drink in his hand. The breeze rippled through his thin hair. He turned to me and looked as if he expected my arrival.

"You are Sam Laska. I saw you on the news," he said.

"I get the feeling you would know me even if I wasn't on television."

"Yes, I have a color copy of your Driver's Licenses, Florida and Illinois." He pronounced the 's' on the end of Illinois and it pissed me off. "So it was you who killed my brother?"

"No, a police officer did."

"Too bad, I would have thanked you. That bastard thought he belonged with my family. He slithered in and expected to be treated as my equal. But he was crude and arrogant. I used that, though. I used the blunt instrument that was Alexei Sanchez. Now he is gone. Have you come to kill me then? My friend would take exception to that." Rutikov looked to the far end of the patio.

A man stepped from a doorway. He was taller than me and powerfully built, like an NFL lineman. His shoulders were twice my width and this biceps stretched the fabric of his suit coat. He stroked his mustache and goatee as he walked over and took a position between Rutikov and myself. He brushed his coat back to show me the pistol on his hip.

"No, I didn't come to kill you," I said. "I came to see the man that destroyed so many lives. And I came to tell you I am responsible for destroying yours."

"Hah! You're wrong, Mr. Laska. My life has not been destroyed. This mountain of a man before you is Mr. Robert Bischkopf. He works for the Governor in a private capacity. The same Governor who will soon wave his magic wand and make all my troubles vanish. You see he understands that my troubles are his troubles. We are tied together at the wallet.

"By this time tomorrow I will be in the Cayman Islands. Not long after that I will return and begin again. The Governor has promised I will never spend a day in prison. It's good to have the most powerful man in the State in one's pocket."

I looked from Rutikov to the stoic Mr. Bischkopf and back again. "Yeah," I said, "I'm from Chicago. You don't need to tell me about corrupt politicians and the things they'll do to protect themselves."

Bischkopf pulled open a sliding glass door that led to the kitchen. "Show yourself out, Mr. Laska," Rutikov said. I walked through the house and out the front door to my car. Before I started the engine I heard a single gunshot echo from the back of the house. The Governor had kept his promise. Marko Rutikov would never face prison.

I drove home, undressed and climbed into bed with Marley. She was still sleeping.

ABOUT THE AUTHOR

The author was born and raised in Chicago, Illinois. He joined the Chicago Police Department in 1977 and served 29 years, retiring in 2006. During his career he was assigned to a wide variety of positions including: Patrol Officer, Tactical Officer, Gang Crime Specialist, Detective, Sergeant, and Lieutenant. The bulk of his career was spent in the Detective Division serving as a Detective, Sergeant, and Lieutenant. At the time of his retirement he was assigned as the Commanding Officer of the Area Three Homicide/Sex Crimes unit on the north side of the city.

Having fallen in love with Florida's gulf coast over the years, he and his wife relocated to the Sarasota area in 2006. Soon after, he began teaching. He shared his expertise and knowledge with his students at a small, private university until 2011 when he retired for a second time.

He and his wife Sharon still live near Sarasota and the crystal sands of Florida's gulf coast.

Made in the USA
Charleston, SC
27 August 2016